I0654128

BEFORE ANYONE FINDS OUT

MARCOS ANTONIO HERNANDEZ

CHAPTER ONE

TOWERS REACHING for the night overlook a lone man walking along the empty streets below, the sound of his boots against the pavement reverberating off their walls. The graffiti covering their lower surfaces represents generations of various signatures and designs fighting for primacy. Neon lights from countless animated billboards on their exterior's upper levels cast flashing multicolored filters through the haze surrounding the man. The graffiti's unaltered colors appear near the occasional working streetlight—reproductions of the palettes popularized by the advertisers on the levels high above.

The Operator pays no attention to the flashing lights cutting through the haze around him. His brown duster swishes around his feet while he walks. He stares forward, unblinking, searching for threats from the world around him through his peripherals. The city's countless rats account for the movement below knee height; their shuffling continues undisturbed as the stranger passes.

It's his first time in the city's Sigma district since he carried out the assassination. The city sees so many murders that nobody bothers remembering who pulled the trigger. Getting lost in the noise is safer than hiding.

The man he's now tracking down came from Gamma. He worked for the district's former chief Enforcer, Bacas, and left the district before the Enforcer's showdown with the Operator in the middle of Gamma's streets.

The Operator turns the corner onto a well-lit street. Every streetlight in this area works—the working bulbs transplanted from the dark street he walked through before. Ahead is a cheering crowd on three sides of two hovercrafts, the street ahead of them wide open. A young woman standing between the two vehicles screams at the top of her lungs while the Operator approaches.

"Three . . . two . . . one . . . go!"

The hovercrafts lurch forward, taking off into the distance, while the crowd screams.

The race is over by the time the Operator gets to the group. A thin, pointed-face man gives out disks to a handful of smiling gamblers who won money on the race while the majority of the people in attendance stare with contempt at the winners.

The Operator approaches a woman standing alone at the fringe, more subdued than the rest. "Excuse me. I'm looking for Nacho," he says.

The woman stares at the Operator with a look of disgust on her face and spits on the ground. The body modification of choice in Sigma is sharpened teeth, and he sees a flash of pointed incisors when she sucks her teeth. "You here to hurt him?"

"Hurt him? No, I just want to talk," the Operator replies.

"You should hurt him. You'd be doing us all a favor. He's taking everyone's money."

The woman reaches out and pulls the Operator forward,

into her, and out of the way of two vehicles approaching the starting line.

"Those look new," the Operator remarks, watching the hovercrafts take their position at the starting line.

"Stolen from the higher-ups," the woman says with a mischievous glint in her eye.

The crowd makes another round of bets with the pointed-face man. One of the winners from before makes his wager last, accompanied by a groan from those who took the opposing competitor.

"That's Nacho," the woman says, pointing to the final gambler, a smiling man with a shaved head, red beard, and beady eyes. The whites of his eyes are colored blue—Gamma district's body modification of choice.

A burly man barks orders at the two drivers from between their taillights. "You know the rules: no more than two meters from the ground, and you wait until you hear go. Anyone who starts early loses."

Both drivers nod.

The vehicles take off after the young girl's countdown. The crowds cheer as if the volume of their voices can propel their chosen candidate to victory. After the race, a flag waves from the right side of the street in the distance; Nacho and the others who won the bet keep cheering.

The Operator walks up to Nacho and stands next to him. The red-bearded man eyes the stranger and inches away. The Operator follows.

"What do you want? I have a girlfriend," Nacho says.

"You came from Gamma district."

"I'm done with that place," Nacho says, flashing his pointed teeth. "I'm Sigma now."

Nacho catches the Operator staring at his eyes and becomes

self-conscious. "Look, man, they don't have a problem with me here. Anything I've got to do with Gamma is in the past."

"I'm told you worked for Bacas."

Nacho's eyes widen for an instant before narrowing. "Who are you?"

"Did you work for him?"

"It's in the past," Nacho says, turning away.

The Operator grabs his wrist. "I'm looking for a girl."

Nacho stares at the hand holding his arm, then glares at the Operator. "I'm not a pimp," he says, ripping his arm away.

"Not that kind of girl. A young girl, held hostage."

Nacho looks at the Operator with a cruel smile on his lips. "I don't know anything about any hostages." He tries walking away, but the Operator grabs onto the back of his jacket.

"Hey!" he yells, loud enough to get the crowd's attention.

Everyone looks at the Operator.

The Operator leans in close to Nacho. "You've been fleecing them. Why would they help you?" he whispers.

Nacho looks around. "You won't have a chance to win your money back if this guy doesn't leave me alone!" he says to the group.

The burly man barking orders and the thin man arranging the bets take one step closer to the Operator and Nacho, their hands meandering to their hips. Maintaining their race's integrity.

The Operator lets go of Nacho and closes his eyes. These aren't security drones, these are flesh-and-blood humans. Or so he thinks. Any androids this far down would be obvious—the high-tech, indistinguishable ones are somewhere dozens of levels above them.

Nacho turns around and smiles at the Operator. "I'm done putting my money down if this guy is around," he says to the organizers.

The burly man steps towards the Operator. The Operator pulls out his blaster and the man steps back and withdraws his own weapon in the same moment. The thin, narrow-faced man in charge of the money draws his blaster as well.

Nacho leans in close to the Operator. "You're outnumbered," he says.

The Operator doesn't take his eyes from the two men. The blaster is in his right hand, an extension of his body at the end of his replaced arm. The new limb, along with replacements for both of his legs, is the result of the fateful shoot-out in Gamma. He hadn't known he was an android before his injuries, and his existence means even less ever since he found out that he was never alive.

But the two men in front of him, they're alive.

The Operator looks at both men. "What should we do?"

The money collector, after a quick glance at the burly man, tells the Operator he can leave if he says sorry.

"I'm not going anywhere. I've got a question for our friend Nacho here," the Operator says, tilting his head in Nacho's direction.

The thin man looks at his partner and shrugs. "Hey, I tried."

"You did," the burly man says.

While the crowd holds their breath, the three men stare at each other until Nacho interrupts. "Just do what you have to do so we can keep racing!" he says to the race's organizers, yelling so the crowd around them becomes involved in the bargain.

"You don't want to do this," the Operator says.

"*We* don't want to? There's two of us, just one of you. What do you think will happen, amigo?"

"This is your last chance. Walk away and let me talk to our lucky friend here."

The narrow-faced man's head tilts to the side. "Where are you even from? You don't have any mods."

"You're right, I don't."

"Then where did you come from?"

"The badlands."

Both men shuffle, their certainty inhibited by a single word, but with their honor on the line they won't back down. All of a sudden, Nacho stammers something about having somewhere else to be and he hurries away towards the finish line.

"Will you let me go after him? He's leaving anyways—no money for you to keep in the pot," the Operator says.

"No! You can go back where you came from," the burly man responds.

The Operator sighs. In the span of a blink, he takes stock of his available options, canceling out those that result in mortal harm to the two men. He lowers his blaster enough that the men in front of him lose their focus, then relaxes every muscle in his body and falls to the ground. He fires two shots in midair, one at the outside of a fleshy thigh and another at a thin upper arm.

Both men fall to the ground, bleeding. The Operator stands, kicks their dropped guns away from their reach, and holsters his own weapon.

"I'm sure they have some money on them," he tells the crowd. Everyone watching drops their chin an inch, their eyes gleaming with avarice, and they rush the two men while the Operator turns and chases after Nacho.

CHAPTER TWO

NACHO SEES THE OPERATOR, below the brightness of a streetlight, turn in his direction and breaks into an all-out run. The Operator, not in the mood for a chase, shakes his head and picks up his pace. His duster trails behind him, caught in the wind as he runs. Ahead, Nacho turns into a dark alley.

The Operator turns the corner and through the darkness witnesses Nacho pull a metal fire escape ladder up to the first floor. Several trash cans lie on their side between him and the ladder, the loose contents spread over the asphalt—a weak attempt at creating an impediment. The men catch each other's glance as Nacho starts up the metal stairs, his steps echoing off the surrounding buildings' walls as the Operator rushes forward.

After standing beneath the ladder and jumping as high as he can, the Operator wraps a few fingers around the bottom rung—enough that when gravity exerts itself he manages a quick hold before his grip slips. His body orients horizontal and he falls, landing on the pavement with a body-shaking thud that takes his breath away. Rolling over to his side with a wheeze, he comes face-to-face with a large rat. The animal's nose wiggles as it sniffs before it turns away in search of food among the trash.

Nacho disappears from the metal steps into a second-story window. The Operator picks himself up and leans back; his spine releases a large crack. His eyes open wide as he waits for any negative outcomes from the shift in his vertebrae. Confident he still feels all his extremities, he takes a few steps back then runs forward. Pushing off the wall with one leg, he catches the ladder and hangs for a brief moment before the ladder starts sliding down. Once his feet hit solid ground, his arms help gravity bring the ladder the rest of the way down. Then, he scrambles up.

The Operator runs up the stairs, which turn at the first level. The window on the second story is cracked open; he rushes in and finds himself in an abandoned manufacturing facility. The thin slivers of light making their way inside combined with his vision adjusting to the darkness reveal stations with archaic, various-sized machines covered in thick layers of dust. Littering the ground are unfinished fabric dolls, some unstuffed, some missing eyes, and others unclothed. On the far side of the space a door slams shut, and the Operator breaks into a jog across the space, shifting his hips as he makes his way around the obstacles.

Halfway across, he jumps over an open box of buttons. One of his feet lands on a compromised piece of flooring and breaks through, sinking him down to his knee. He waits for a moment with half of one leg beneath the floor, his other foot on solid ground with a bent knee and both hands on the floor, preparing for a fall if the rest of the floor gives way. The ground around him shifts, sinking him still further, and he wrenches his leg out and pushes away with his other three limbs, lunging as far forward as he can, ending up sprawled out in the dust. With one final shift, the floor where he was a moment before drops out and lands on the level below with a loud crash, leaving him dangling from his armpits. He shifts left to right, gathering momentum each time, and on his third swing he hooks his right leg on the floor, pulling himself up with the added leverage.

After rushing through the door where Nacho disappeared, the Operator finds himself in a long hallway running the width of the factory, perpendicular to the threshold. On his near left, three doors away, is a barred window. Assuming Nacho wouldn't go this way, the Operator turns right and walks forward, listening. He leans in close and listens for rustling at each door he passes. They're empty. A loud crash rings out from outside the window behind him; he turns and runs to the barred window and looks outside. There, on the cracked asphalt below, Nacho stands over a metal trash can. Something pulls the pursued man's gaze up to the window on the second story and he runs when he sees the Operator staring down at him, disappearing into an adjoining side street.

The Operator pulls at the window. It's stuck, but with a quick yank it opens. He grabs the metal bars beyond the glass and tugs—they don't move. Stepping back, he tries kicking them, but they're unyielding. Instead of struggling with the bars, the Operator turns and runs down the hall, looking for a staircase. He finds one halfway down the hall and runs down, clearing two steps at a time.

The door leading to the street below is wide open. The Operator runs through, clears the tipped-over metal can with a bound, and turns down the side street, finding that it ends in an overgrown courtyard. Centered between the towering buildings is a decrepit playground covered with vines, surrounded by a low concrete wall on all four sides with spaces left open on the corners. On the far side of the courtyard is a bright red door, and next to the door is a window with a smiling Nacho peering out.

He waves and makes a gun with his fingers, pointing it at the Operator.

The courtyard's other entrance is on the far right corner. The Operator is about to rush to the red door when movement draws his attention. Men are marching forward, two at a time, guns drawn. The Operator ducks behind a concrete wall, pulls out his own weapon, and pokes his head and arm up, aiming at them. The men's faces remain blank as they march.

In a flash of inspiration, the Operator realizes they aren't men—they're androids. Old versions too, from their mechanical movements and lack of awareness. Each one's clothes could pass for anyone at the street race. The Operator puts his back to the barrier and chuckles to himself. This shouldn't take any time at all.

His smile disappears when the shooting begins. Their erratic shots hit different areas of the concrete barrier he's hiding behind, and as the shooting intensifies, he wonders how lucky he's feeling that day. He crawls to the side farthest from their entrance and peeks around the end of the barrier. Dozens of androids are shooting where he was before. Concrete chips fly in every direction.

Taking aim, he shoots the heads off seven androids before he retreats when the rest of the group realizes his position has changed. They begin decimating the concrete where his head was one moment before.

Understanding their primitive processing, and annoyed with Nacho for thinking this model poses any threat, the Operator crawls to the other side of the barrier, the side closest to their entrance, and pokes his head out. To his surprise, some of the androids have moved forward while shooting where he was, and he takes out those closest to him before the group turns their focus on his new location and he takes cover once more.

Then, while they're shooting the concrete near the ground

where he was, the Operator crawls to the other side of the barrier and rushes forward to the other side of the playground's square enclosure, passing the open space between the barriers. While he crawls, a shot lands on the asphalt near his hand, and he turns and sees an android, his eyes dull and face blank, standing atop the slide. The Operator shoots him between the eyes before scrambling forward. The android collapses and begins a slow descent down the slide with a screech from his artificial skin on the smooth surface.

He has a full view of the group from his new position. They still stand in pairs, but now he has their broad side. The Operator makes quick work of the wave closest to him, decimating half the ranks with one round of shots. When the remaining androids determine his position, he ducks down and scurries forward before preparing for the final volley. With a breath, he stands up. As concrete flies from where he fired the previous round, he takes aim and pulls the trigger.

Nothing happens.

"Not now!" he says, drawing attention to his new position. He ducks down, places his back against the concrete barrier, and hits the heel of his palm with the side of the gun. A shot erupts from the barrel after a few hits, making a hole next to his foot.

The Operator closes his eyes and takes a deep breath, calming himself. Tired of crawling, he wants this gunfight over with so he can talk with Nacho. He turns around the end of the barricade, coming up to full height, and starts shooting as he runs towards the red door. Within moments, the remaining androids are all standing headless. Then, they all collapse as one, leaving the Operator alone in the courtyard.

The red door opens with one swift, well-placed kick. Nacho stands inside an empty, graffitied room, sweating, with his hands up. He smiles when the Operator takes aim at his chest.

"I think there's been a misunderstanding," Nacho says.

The Operator points to a chair with his gun. "Sit," he says.

Nacho sits down. The Operator, never taking his eyes off Nacho, finds a chair on the other side of the room, moves it across from Nacho, and sits down as well.

"What can I do for you?" Nacho asks, as if he was in the room waiting for the Operator's appointment all along.

"Bacas kept a young girl hostage. The daughter of a doctor—"

"Yes, I remember," Nacho says. He pauses. "Gabi. That was her name, I think. Gabi. What about her?"

"What happened to her?"

"How should I know? She was staying in the apartments above his casino when I left."

The Operator moves his gun from the man's chest to his groin.

"Hey, I'm telling you the truth! He just kept her in the room the entire time, said the doc would do whatever he wanted as long as the girl was kept safe!"

The gun continues down and ends up pointed at the ground.

"Are you her father?" Nacho asks.

The Operator laughs to himself—Nacho has no idea that he's talking to an android. To be fair, he didn't know either, not until his three limb replacements. "No, but I'm looking for her."

"I can help!" Nacho says, pleading. "I know Gamma like the back of my hand."

"I don't need anyone's help," the Operator says, standing up.

He turns towards the door—it's brown on the inside, in sharp contrast to the bright red seen from outside. Walking forward, he hears a quick rustling, turns while pulling his blaster back up, and sees Nacho's hand withdrawing a pistol from an ankle holster.

The Operator shoots the arm holding the pistol at the wrist and the hand drops away, the weapon with it. Instead of blood and bone fragments, the end of the arm is sparking, crackling wires.

"My hand!" Nacho screams, his left hand clutching his right forearm.

The Operator looks at the gleaming machinery. "You should hide that, before someone finds out," he says, before walking out the door.

CHAPTER THREE

GAMMA DISTRICT never looked so beautiful. Nothing had changed while the Operator was in Sigma, but being back among people with the whites of their eyes replaced by a vivid blue comforts him, despite his lack of participation with the practice. He's home.

Changing the color of his own eyes never crossed his mind before he learned he was an android, and nothing changed after. Fitting in isn't high on his agenda. Changing the color of his eyes, sharpening his teeth, or removing his nostrils like the people in Theta is now easier for him as an android, since reversal is as simple as replacing the changed aspect of his body. But he enjoys not outright belonging to any district, calling anywhere he lays his head his home.

He walks down the street with his typical measured cadence, aware of everything around him and confident he can handle any threats. The rats run rampant in this district too—over the entire city, in fact, since messenger rats are the sole source of surveillance-free communication available to the residents below the reclaimers—but there's something about

Gamma's rats that makes them seem more refined than the ones in Sigma.

Gamma's residents stare at the Operator as he walks by them in the early morning haze. The younger adults are still out from the night before, and the older residents peek out from behind windows on the first three levels. The reclaimers above the third level are the demarcation line that separates the lowest humans on the rung from those on the higher levels. The persistent haze close to the ground disappears past the reclaimers and provides the upper levels with clean air. The companies who pay for the massive neon billboards, some of which take up entire buildings, are the strongest supporters of reclaimer maintenance, ensuring the people who can afford their products can see their advertisements from a distance and keep them in mind whenever they open their wallets.

The pool hall the Operator calls home is halfway between the line where Gamma district begins and the city's edge. The skeleton of his broken-down hovercraft, the one he rode in on from the badlands, sits outside, stripped for parts. A pit in his stomach forms when he thinks about Fenix, the dog he brought in from the badlands with him; any positive feelings associated with his former companion dissipate—replaced by anger—when he remembers how Bacas, Gamma's chief Enforcer below the third, shot him. Shaking his head, he makes his way to the open pool hall door.

He pauses. The door shouldn't be open. They fixed the door during his recuperation, when he was still getting used to his new limbs. And the pool hall shouldn't be open for business at this time—anyone staying late in the night would have been kicked out hours before.

The Operator pushes the cracked door open farther with his right hand, peering in through the widening space. Four people are inside: three young men, two playing pool and the third sitting in a chair, his feet on another pool table, with a blaster pointed at the pool hall's owner.

"Welcome back," the pool hall owner, Miguel, says. He's wearing his typical outfit: a dark brown button-down shirt, frayed jeans, and ancient, once-white sneakers.

"Thanks," the Operator says, closing the door behind him.

The pool game stops and both men stand tall, their cue sticks resting on the floor. "This place is closed," one of them says.

The Operator takes off his duster and places it on the coatrack next to the front door—another new installation.

The two men playing pool look at their seated comrade for direction. The one sitting down doesn't move his blaster from Miguel's direction. He nods towards the Operator.

Both cue sticks become weapons at the head movement. The Operator lets out a sigh of relief when they don't crack them in half—he had no idea cue sticks were so expensive when they started renovating the pool hall.

Brandishing the sticks, the two men stand between the Operator and Miguel, telling the new arrival that he should leave before things get ugly.

Miguel laughs behind them. "Things are definitely going to get ugly," he says. He steps back from the bar, resting his back-side on the counter behind him.

The Operator looks at the two men threatening him, one at a time. One's angry, the other nervous. He lifts his hands in front of him, and instead of making fists, he opens his palms and shrugs.

The angry one rushes forward and takes a wild downward swing. The Operator sidesteps, aware of where the cue stick is throughout the swing as if the attack is in slow motion. His right hand shoots forward, grips the back of the man's shirt, and adds to his momentum, sending him crashing into the doorframe headfirst.

The nervous one, preparing for the altercation, takes deep, stimulating breaths, his shoulders rising and falling in time with his chest. He steps forward and takes a horizontal swing at the Operator, who ducks.

"Look, you don't want to do this, kid," the Operator says.

The nervousness dissipates, replaced by rage. Two more wild horizontal swings later, which the Operator steps back from, and the Operator's back is against the closed door. The second attacker shifts as he regains consciousness.

The Operator bends over and picks up the dropped cue stick during yet another wild swing. As he comes up, he drives it between the attacker's arms, which freezes the young man for a split second. The Operator's left hand reaches up, grabs the top of the stick, and yanks it down, spinning it and breaking the young man's grip. With his right hand, the stronger hand, the Operator pulls the cue stick away from his attacker.

The Operator sets both sticks down, still intact, on the closest pool table. The enraged attacker breathes heavily while helping his partner up, and both of them take a step forward in the Operator's direction. Before they can reach him, or the seated young man can turn his blaster away from Miguel, the Operator has his own blaster out and pointed at their leader.

"We didn't mean anything by it," the leader of the trio says, lowering his weapon to his side.

"Leave it on the table," the Operator says.

The young man's face hardens while weighing his options. In the end he does as he's told.

He stands with his hands in the air. The two attackers, their anger fueled by embarrassment, stare at the Operator, unmoving, while the third member of their group walks past. Realizing they haven't moved, the leader reaches across the two of them with his left hand and ushers them out. Before he shuts the door, the one in charge looks at Miguel.

"He won't always be here to protect you," he says.

The door shuts, and the Operator turns to his friend, the man who first gave him shelter when he came to the city then let him stay. The one who replaced his limbs and helped him get used to them. "Have they been here all night?" he asks, approaching the bar.

"Came in right before close," Miguel says, wiping a glass.

"That can wait, go to bed," the Operator says, looking at the glass.

"I'm wide awake after all that, amigo. Any luck finding the girl?"

The Operator pulls a stool away from the bar and sits down. "Found the informant easily enough, he was right in the thick of things at the race. But he ran when I asked him what he knew, and tried using early-android security against me."

Miguel laughs. "Did you leave any of them intact?"

"What do you think?" the Operator says.

Miguel chuckles and holds the glass up, inspecting it for smudges. Satisfied, he sets it back down with the other clean glasses.

"So did you talk to him? Find out where she is?"

"He said he has no idea where she is. I found out her name though: Gabi."

"Gabi," Miguel says, weighing the word on his tongue. "He didn't say anything about where she could be?"

"Not a thing. He did say she was in the apartments above Suerte when he worked for Bacas. Maybe one of the people in the building knows where she went?"

"Those were all Bacas's men. You could try, but I doubt it."

"Best lead I've got."

Miguel pours a glass of Serum, the popular Stim alternative

below the reclaimers, and passes it to the Operator. He takes a swig and feels his muscles release their tension, accompanied by a familiar sense of clarity. Unlike Stim, Serum's not addictive and doesn't provide abundant energy that requires physical movement. If Stim is a slap to the face, Serum is a splash with tepid water.

"Well, you're one step closer to leaving the city behind. You know, you could always leave without finding the girl . . ."

"Her mother saved my life. I'm not leaving before my debt is paid. Besides, who's going to protect you from these thugs?" the Operator says with a nod to the door.

"Oh, them? They would've gotten bored, eventually."

The Operator shakes his head.

"If I was all those men, I wouldn't want to deal with a little girl without Bacas telling me to," Miguel says, thinking out loud. "I'd probably send her to the orphanage."

"There are orphanages?" the Operator says, one hand resting on his glass.

"They aren't the best places in the world, but each district has one."

"Who pays for it?"

"Government. Same people who pay for the Enforcers. From what I've heard, same level of corruption runs through 'em too."

"Why didn't you mention this before?" the Operator says, his head tilting to the side with simmering disbelief.

"Didn't think to," Miguel replies. "And what would you have said if you showed up there? 'I'm looking for a girl. Don't know her age, or her name.' They would've looked at you like you're crazy!"

"Well, now that I've got a name it shouldn't be too hard to check if she's there."

"Exactly. Do you even know how old she is?"

"Not a clue." The Operator downs the remaining Serum and stands up.

"Where are you going?" Miguel asks.

"To check the orphanage . . ."

"Amigo, the city's just waking up! They won't let you in for a few more hours." Miguel turns around. "Relax, be patient. There's nothing you can do right now."

Somehow, the thought of relaxing sounds more intimidating than facing a trio of intruders.

CHAPTER FOUR

THE ORPHANAGE IS around the corner from Suerte, the casino Bacas owned before the Operator ended the Enforcer's life. It takes up the second and third levels of a building: the workers and support facilities on the second floor, the children housed on the third.

The staircase's exit on the second floor doubles as the orphanage's entrance. The Operator walks through, expecting greeting from a sea of rowdy children. He finds silence instead. He walks down the hallway leading away from the entrance, peeking into each room he passes. A health room on his left has two doors leading into it, and for a span of five doors on his right is a cafeteria, a long table running the length of the space. Past the health room on the left is another large space with multiple doors leading into it: a recreation room. The last rooms in the hall are classrooms, complete with chalkboards and dozens of small desks.

Yelling trickles through the door at the end of the hall. "Come on, lots to do today!" a woman's voice says from far away.

The Operator goes through the door and climbs the stairs

beyond, finding himself behind a lone woman facing the hall. Various-aged children emerge from their rooms beyond her, their eyes puffy and hair sticking out at odd angles.

"Excuse me," the Operator says.

Startled, the woman turns around, her brown hair brushing past her shoulders. "You scared me!" she says. "Are you the replacement?" she asks, hopeful. Despite her youth, she has deep circles around her eyes, which stand in sharp contrast to her pale skin.

"No, I'm looking for someone."

The woman's shoulders sag, defeated. "Alone again today."

"Alone? With all these kids?"

She nods. Then, turning back around, she yells, "Hurry up!" Her attention back on the Operator, she explains with a smile how they never listen to her.

"I'm looking for a girl named Gabi."

"Gabi? She isn't here," the woman says.

"Where is she?"

The woman's eyes narrow. "Why do you need to find her?"

"I made a promise to her mother," the Operator says.

"Her mother? We never knew anything about her. She just showed up one day. Smartest kid we've had in here, though she never talked much—she already knew everything we were learning about."

The Operator nods. Behind the woman, a young boy with a wicked smile walks out of the bathroom with a roll of toilet paper. After confirming the woman still has her back turned, he holds the loose end and throws the rest of the roll down the hall, watching it unfurl. "And she's not here anymore?" he asks.

"No, I managed to get her transferred to the upper orphanage, the one for the third through tenth. They have more staff there, and have the time to actually teach her new things, since she's so much further along than the other children here."

The children fall silent while they watch the toilet paper roll the length of the hallway. Getting a sense that mischief is underway from the sudden lack of noise, the woman turns around. "Tommy!" she yells while rushing forward. Remembering the Operator, she turns around and tells him she's sorry. "I wish I could help more."

"Last question," the Operator says.

She snatches the end of the toilet paper from Tommy's hand and tells him to get dressed. "Make it quick."

"What level is the other orphanage on?"

"Seven," she says, rushing off towards the far end of the hallway where the toilet paper roll's progress has stopped at the wall.

"Thanks," the Operator says with a nod, doubtful the harried woman heard him. He turns around and leaves the struggling orphanage.

Back on the street outside the building, the Operator paces, with the occasional glance to the higher levels. A flashing billboard catches his eye, an electronics brand he hasn't thought of in years: Takahari. The pink neon cursive letters appear one at a time, the complete word flashes twice, then the process begins again. Every time he passes below the reclaimers, he swears he's never going above them again. And now another situation pulls him back up, back to what he left behind all those years ago.

And this time, he doesn't have forged documents.

His attention returns to the ground level when he realizes a group of diners are watching his deliberation. Their chosen restaurant is little more than a counter with a dingy sign above a tattered red-and-yellow awning. Their high-top tables are without seats—the diners stand while they eat from white paper boxes. The restaurant shares the dining area with another establishment, one that belongs to the next street over, and the Operator can see clear through the shared open space to the building on the next block.

The people watching the Operator slurp their noodles without taking their eyes off him. He waves without smiling and they nod their heads in response. The restaurant owner, noticing the Operator looking inside, yells out about how he has the best noodles in town.

"We have a special, today only—buy one, get one free! You'll regret it if you don't!"

The Operator shakes his head and walks away.

Accessing the first three floors, the ones below the reclaimers, is straightforward enough: walk up the stairs and hope nobody gives you any trouble. Living there is another matter. Most people below the reclaimers don't find any value in spending more for a home on a higher level still below the clean air, which means most people live on the ground floor. The sensors at the third level make sure nobody accesses the clean air above the third-level reclaimers without paying the proper taxes.

The Operator, in a past life, lived on the fifty-second level. He doesn't have his ID card, but he should still be in the database. The crossing is filled with people waiting to head up through the staircase on the far wall; nobody travels in the opposite direction. He takes his place in line and watches as the people ahead of him get sent back by a single face-mask-wearing guard in a khaki jumpsuit. There are three other guards in the crossing station—wearing matching black face masks and hats, in addition to the standard khaki garb—dispersed through the crowd. Some of the turned-away travelers plead with the guard making the decision, appealing to his humanity, and some insist there's been a mistake. One of them, a pregnant woman, begs for the chance for her child to be born above the reclaimers.

"The air . . . it'll be better for her lungs!" she cries.

"Children are born below all the time," the guard escorting her out snarls back, shoving her. She stumbles into the Operator, who makes sure she doesn't fall.

The pregnant woman gathers herself, thanks the Operator, then turns around and yells, "I'll be back tomorrow!"

She walks back to the lower levels in a huff.

The guard checking credentials doesn't permit a single person through; one of his comrades keeps a close watch on the Operator. The guard believes his glances are unnoticed while he continues making his rounds, but the Operator tracks him out of his peripherals. When the guard stops next to another among the crowd and whispers something to him, both men look at the Operator before the one who heard the secret shakes his head. The Operator keeps his eyes forward while he waits for his turn.

"Next!" the guard checking credentials says.

The Operator steps forward.

"Identification?"

"I don't have it."

"Well then why are you wasting my time? Get out of here!"

"I'm in the database."

The guard raises his eyebrows. "The database? Like the above-ten database?" He looks at the Operator for a moment, inspecting his dirty brown duster and overall haggard appearance, before erupting into laughter. "I'm sure you are!"

The Operator doesn't laugh. Doesn't even smile. He just waits.

"Get him out of here!" the laughing guard says.

The guard who heard the whispered secret steps forward and puts a hand on the Operator's shoulder. The Operator stares at the contact, then turns to the one making decisions. "Get out the scanner."

The two guards nearest the Operator look at each other and

laugh. "This guy's got guts!" the one checking credentials says. He reaches underneath the desk and pulls out a handheld machine with a square display—the attached cushion has an eye-sized hole in the center. "Lean in here, then," he says.

The Operator rips his shoulder forward, away from the guard's grip, then leans in, putting his eye into the scanner. The machine beeps a second later, and the Operator pulls back with a stunned guard in front of him.

"Fifty . . . fifty-two," the guard stammers. He stares, confused. "What are you doing all the way down here?"

"Can I go through now?"

The guard nods, then pushes a button. Ahead, the clear door that separates the space opens. The Operator walks forward without a glance back.

"Stop!" someone says when the Operator's foot is on the staircase's first step.

The Operator, not thinking the orders are for him, continues.

"Fifty-two! Stop!"

The Operator pauses with one foot on the second step, one foot on the third. He turns around and sees all four guards with their blasters aimed at him. "Is there something wrong?" he says.

"I remember where I recognize you from," the guard who was glancing at the Operator says. He takes off his hat and exposes a head full of blond hair.

Ludavico. One of Bacas's men. A gang member without a leader, forced to go corporate. Time hasn't been kind to the man.

"So you didn't die," the Operator says.

"My brother did. You killed him."

The Operator nods while pulling his arms through his duster as if he's arriving for a visit and making himself comfortable. "You two look a lot alike."

"What are you doing?" Ludavico's brother snaps.

"I'm hot," the Operator says.

"Stop moving or I'll shoot!"

The Operator finishes pulling his duster off, then drapes it over his arm. "So what do you propose we do?"

"You're coming with us."

"That's not happening," the Operator whispers, shaking his head. In one swift movement, he tosses his long jacket up in such a way that it opens up wide as he turns around and runs up the stairs. Blasters shoot through the fabric, taking out chunks from the stairs where his feet were moments before.

CHAPTER FIVE

FOOTSTEPS FOLLOW the Operator as he sprints up the stairs. He listens while he runs, guessing that there are two on his tail—the other two having stayed back at the checkpoint. The fourth and fifth levels pass with the same distance between him and his pursuers. With a pang of regret, the Operator realizes he misses the familiar swish of his duster trailing off of his back.

The Operator turns off the staircase on the sixth level, erupting into a large room the size of a convention hall—with any luck, the guards assume he's kept climbing until they arrive at the next checkpoint on the tenth. There are hundreds of stalls selling everything from food to clothing. Hundreds of inhabitants from the fourth through tenth stroll through the aisles, shopping at their section's bazaar. The Operator plunges into the crowd, walking away from the door as fast as he can without breaking into a run, with the occasional backwards glance at the nondescript door he burst through.

A shock of blond hair and black face mask appears through the door during the Operator's second glance back. The guard scans the room, then disappears back through the door. The Operator slows his walk and notices the sideways glances of the people around him. With his black long-sleeved shirt, black pants held up by silver suspenders, silver belt and holster, and black boots, he stands in stark contrast to the well-dressed people shopping in the bazaar. The other men are dressed in bright colors, some wearing robes and some sporting blazers and slacks—yellow is the most common color. The women in the crowd are the ones dressed in black. The Operator ignores their looks while he searches for an exit.

He turns around one last time, a final check if he's being followed, and sees both guards burst through the door. Ludavico's brother and the Operator catch each other's eyes, and the guard resumes his running pursuit, his comrade following behind. The Operator groans then starts weaving through the crowd as fast as his legs can carry him.

The row of stalls ends at an open space on the far side of the hall. A zigzagging line of people wait outside a wall of bay doors with a single word written above them: MEAT. A pair of guards, wearing the same government-issued wardrobe as the ones from the checkpoint chasing him, stands outside the third bay door, handing out frozen meat, with water vapor trailing around their feet. Each person in line receives one frozen portion after having their face scanned for payment. The two doors on the right are wide open, their containers empty, but the numerous doors on the left are still closed, with metal locks hanging from their closing mechanisms. Making sure his pursuers see him turn right at the end of the stalls, the Operator runs around the side of the crowd, turns to the left, and runs across the space between the masses and the frozen storage containers, hidden from the checkpoint's guards by the people in line. He withdraws his gun and shoots the locks of the three containers next to the meat guards. They don't move—protecting the available meat is their first priority. On the fourth container, with the meat guards calling for backup, he stops and opens the freezer door after shooting the lock, exposing the frozen meat to the crowd.

"Come and get it!" he yells.

The people closest to the Operator look at each other for a second, as frozen in place as the meat they're waiting for, before the dam bursts and they rush forward, filling the space between the meat guards and the Operator. By the time the final locks are shot away, members of the crowd stand near the unopened containers, ready to throw open the doors after the Operator passes.

Now on the left side of the wall of meat containers, the Operator hurries into the surrounding stalls, telling everyone he finds that there's free meat available. He stands next to a wall and watches a nearby shop owner alternate his attention between the clothes he sells and the growing crowd around the meat. The shop owner decides he can't ignore the opportunity for free meat and leaves his clothes behind, and the Operator emerges from his hidden position, approaches the stall, and grabs a hooded black shawl and throws it over his back.

The Operator inspects the area behind the crowd, where the guards chasing him from the checkpoint stand scanning the madness in front of them. They split up, one man going to the right side and the blond-haired brother going to the left, towards the Operator. The Operator doesn't run. Instead, he keeps his head down, with his shoulder hunched, and flips through the available clothes. Out of the corner of his eye, he sees the guard rush by, his gun drawn.

After a moment, the Operator walks away from the clothing stall, still hunched and looking at the ground, and retraces his steps back to the staircase. A hand grips his shoulder and spins him around when he's mere steps from exiting the bazaar. The Operator comes face-to-face with a graying man with dense eyebrows and a weak jaw.

"Sorry," the man says, stumbling backwards and over his words at the same time. "I thought you were my wife."

The Operator smiles, his head still bent towards the ground, and looks at the man from the tops of his eyes. "You really shouldn't grab *anyone* like that," he says.

The graying man's face hardens. "Don't tell me how I should be treating people," he says, seething.

"I'll be watching," the Operator says with a wink before flashing his gun.

The man lifts both hands and backs away, his head on a swivel, searching for his wife.

The Operator takes off the black shawl once he's in the stairwell. He climbs to the seventh level with the garment slung over his arm. He pauses before walking through the door, delighting in the silence from below.

The door from the stairway onto the seventh level opens into a row of aged classroom doors. They extend far into the distance to the left and right, the same length as the convention hall beneath, with dingy markers on the ceiling denoting the various hallways that cut across. The Operator peeks into each room through a sliver of a window above the door handle, catching the eyes of students sitting at secondhand desks while their teacher speaks in front of the classroom. One group of students, their teacher's back turned, points at him, and he puts a finger to his lips before moving on.

"What are you doing here?" a shrill voice says from down the hall.

The Operator stands tall. "I have a donation, for the teachers," he says, holding out the shawl, and the inquiring woman approaches him.

"A donation?" The woman takes the shawl from the Operator and inspects it. "You came here just to give us . . . a shawl?"

"I did."

"Thank you?" the woman says, her suspicious eyes searching the Operator's face. The top of her curled gray hair reaches the Operator's shoulder, and a generous helping of makeup hides her wrinkles whenever she isn't talking. "But you really shouldn't be here," she says, gesturing with one arm out behind her. "I'll show you out."

"There is one other thing," the Operator says, unmoving. "I'm looking for a girl named Gabi. I knew her mother."

"We don't allow visitors."

The Operator waits. The woman runs her hand through the gifted shawl and her face relaxes. "Unless you're interested in adopting her?"

"I am," the Operator says. "If she'll have me."

The woman flashes a wicked smile, no longer confrontational. "Let me take you to her."

The Operator follows the orphanage worker through a series of turns to her office, where she searches on her computer. "Ah yes, she's in the twelve-year-old cohort," she says, before leading the Operator to a recreational room.

The children are playing on a miniature obstacle course. Some are talking in small groups, and some are racing through obstacles, all under the watchful eye of a young man wearing a bright green tracksuit.

"Where's Gabi?" the woman barks at the instructor.

The man points to the far corner, where a young girl sits by herself. She's hugging her knees and staring at the other children, her shoulder-length brown hair tucked behind her ears.

The woman leads the Operator around the wall, far out of the way of the playing children, who ignore the visitors. Gabi doesn't look at them as they approach.

The woman stands over the young girl. "Gabi."

The girl looks at the woman out of the corners of her eyes without moving her head.

"This man's here to take you. He knew your mother."

Gabi looks back at the other children.

The woman reaches down, grabs Gabi's wrist, and lifts her to standing. "Look, we've got enough children on our hands as it is, so if someone wants to take you, you better appreciate it!"

The Operator places a hand on the woman's forearm. She lets go, and he takes a knee.

"Your mother saved my life."

Gabi's gaze doesn't leave the playing children ahead of her.

"Let's grab your things and go." He extends a hand to Gabi.

"Don't—" the orphanage worker begins, becoming quiet when she sees the Operator's glare directed at her.

Gabi reaches up and takes the Operator's hand.

The orphanage worker leads them to Gabi's bed, the bottom level of a bunk bed among dozens of others. The sheets are threadbare, and the cracked floor has ancient stains. "I'll be back in a minute," the orphanage worker says, leaving the Operator and Gabi alone.

"Gather your stuff," the Operator says.

Gabi grabs two shirts, two pairs of pants, two pairs of socks, and two pairs of underwear. She opens up one of the shirts, a long-sleeved one, ties the bottom, and stuffs the undergarments inside. Then, she places the pants and other shirt in the middle and ties the arms together. When she's done, she stands in front of the Operator with her makeshift bundle held in one hand.

"Is that it?" the Operator asks.

Gabi nods.

"You really don't have anything else?"

She closes her eyes and shakes her head.

The woman reappears. "Are you ready to go?" she says to Gabi, full of cheer.

Gabi ignores her.

"Ungrateful," the woman spits out. "Let's get you out of here."

The Operator doesn't bother speaking out against the woman, knowing he and Gabi won't be there much longer.

The woman walks the pair down the hall to the main entrance. There, talking with the receptionist at the front desk, is a man in glasses and black overcoat, wearing a white shirt and black tie, surrounded by unblinking, unmoving men in gray compression suits carrying blaster pistols.

Android security. The Operator stops walking. "How did they find me?" he says, thinking out loud. Then, in a flash of inspiration, he asks the woman if she called anyone.

"They told me to call if anyone came looking for Gabi!" the orphanage worker says, her voice heavy with desperation. "You'll still take her, right?"

The Operator grabs Gabi by the shoulder, turns around, and runs.

CHAPTER SIX

"I DIDN'T KNOW!" is the last thing the Operator hears the woman say before he's turning down a hall and heading back in the direction of the stairs. He's almost to the end of the hall when a shot whizzes past his head and lands on one of the signs hanging down from the ceiling ahead of him. Glancing back before he turns, he sees a group of men running down the hall, the stiffness in their joints betraying circuits in place of veins. Behind them, his arms crossed, is the man in glasses.

The Operator turns left, yanking Gabi. She drops her bundle.

"My clothes!" she yells, pulling back against the Operator's grip.

"Leave them," the Operator grunts.

She doesn't listen. Setting her feet, she leans back, generating as much resistance as her light body can manage.

The Operator looks at the bundle, wondering for a split second if he could grab the clothes in time, before he picks Gabi up and throws her over his shoulder. He makes it to the stairs, back to where he gained access to the orphanage in the first place. His feet fly as they strike each stair in rapid succession,

MARCOS ANTONIO HERNANDEZ

rattling Gabi. Her hair covers her face. Recovering from her initial shock, she pounds the Operator's back with her fists, demanding he put her down.

"I'll scream!" she threatens.

It works. The Operator sets her down. Before she has time to fix her hair, he grabs her wrist and pulls her along, making her run faster than she's comfortable going. They go through the door that accesses the bazaar, turn right, and run around the room's exterior until they are at the end of the stalls on the right side of the area for meat purchases.

By now, the meat guards have reinforcements. Together, they've reestablished order. A line of people—smaller than the previous—waits outside a refrigerated unit on the far left side. The Operator runs across the space towards the unit on the far right.

"Hey!" a guard yells out. "You can't go in there!"

The girl inspects the guard while the Operator pulls her into the first refrigerated unit. Then, the Operator closes the door behind them.

They make their way to the front of the unit in darkness. There's a small door at the front—the Operator runs his hands over the surface until he finds the handle and pulls, opening the door to the cab of an industrial hovercraft.

The city beyond the windshield is in full view through the clean air above the reclaimers. It's been so long since the Operator's seen the sight that he stares at the buildings beyond the hovercrafts whizzing by, inspecting the neon-colored advertisements taking up their facades. The vehicles in the zone midway between buildings engage in horizontal travel, and the ones closest to the buildings in the distance travel along the vertical axis. Some are new models, sleek, pointed, single-occupant vehicles in metallic colors, and some are older, wide barge-style models he's surprised still run.

"What are you doing in here?" the driver of the vehicle asks.

"Get out," the Operator says.

"Look, this vehicle's my responsibility; it's under my name. Even if the boss doesn't kill me, I'll never get another job!"

The Operator pulls his blaster out and points it at the man's head. "Tell him it's not your fault."

The driver unbuckles himself with shaking hands, then tries getting past the Operator to the cargo area.

"That way's blocked," the Operator says.

"What do you want me to do then?" the driver asks, his voice quivering.

The Operator gestures with his gun to the side door. There's nothing but air between the door and the vehicle supporting the next refrigerated cargo unit on their left.

The driver's eyes widen. "You can't be serious."

"Now."

A rush of wind enters when the driver opens the door, blowing Gabi's hair away from her face.

"I won't make it," the driver says.

"Try," the Operator replies.

With a gun still in his face and no options left, the driver turns around and, with one hand holding on to his former vehicle, leans out while reaching forward with his other hand. He takes a few quick breaths in rapid succession, then jumps.

The driver hits the vehicle's side and slides down, his hands searching for something to hold. He grabs on to the metal step outside the passenger door. A face appears in the window above the man, looking down. When the other driver realizes someone's hanging on to his vehicle, and sees the Operator and Gabi in the one next to him, he opens the door, reaches down, and pulls his fellow driver up to safety.

The Operator slams the door shut and sits down; Gabi sits in the passenger seat. He searches the interior until he finds a heavy latch hidden within a sea of buttons, dials, and miniature screens, which he pulls. The hovercraft decouples from the refrigeration unit with a scrape of metal on metal, and the Operator urges the craft forward, making a sharp right when they get to the zone for horizontal travel.

The industrial hovercraft, taller than it is wide or long, sticks out among the sleeker models traveling in the same vicinity. In addition to the different size, the other crafts come in various colors and patterns, but the freighter is stark white with a few black scuff marks.

The Operator looks around, searching for a landmark he recognizes. It's been years since he's seen the city from outside a building without the haze below the reclaimers, and he doesn't know the area. He finds the Takahari sign and realizes he's still over Gamma. He's about to edge closer to the nearby building and begin downward vertical travel when flashing lights show up in his rearview mirror.

"Stop where you are!" a voice says through a speaker in the dashboard. It's the police, with access to the communication systems in the freighter.

The Operator looks at Gabi. "We didn't hear that," he says. Then, he pulls out his blaster and shoots the speaker. He checks both of his rearview mirrors, counts six cruisers in pursuit. He knows the beast he's driving won't beat them in a chase. Outrunning them isn't an option. But he won't stop and make their job easier for them.

He continues at a lazy, relaxed speed, traveling along the highway towards Sigma while drivers ahead pull to the left and right after seeing the approaching flashing lights. It's the slowest hovercraft chase the city's ever seen.

Two police vehicles turn onto their path ahead. The Operator doesn't slow down when they appear, and continues forward as they turn to their side. Their windows roll down and two large barrels appear, one from each.

"Are you buckled up?" the Operator says, strapping himself in.

Gabi reaches for the seat belt, pulls it across herself, and joins the clasping mechanism. It doesn't click.

"It doesn't work," Gabi says, her voice betraying her nerves. She tries again, slamming the mechanism together.

The freighter gets closer to the barrels. "Hurry," the Operator says.

Gabi becomes frantic. "I'm trying!"

The Operator counts down from three in his head, extending the space between the numbers more than he would if he were speaking. After one, he tells Gabi to hold on.

The Operator plunges his craft forward and down. At the same instant, the officers who set up in their path fire their charged spears and hit two of the cruisers chasing the Operator, disabling their electronics and tethering themselves together. Gabi loses her grasp on the seat belt and flies to the roof, her upper back hitting the ceiling as she's pinned.

Four functional police cars drop towards the ground; the other four stay suspended in midair.

The Operator swerves between three levels of traffic, dodging traveling hovercrafts on his way to the haze beneath the reclaimers. The cruisers stay hot on his tail.

The colors from the billboard become muted below the third level. The Operator pulls the craft out of its plunge and brings it level with the ground below, translating the generated speed into forward movement. Gabi comes down from the ceiling and hits the seat with her knees, her head going into the space where her feet were during their initial escape. She reorients herself and brushes her hair from her face in a huff.

When acclimated to the haze, it never seems dark. But after coming from the clear air above the reclaimers, the haze now pushes in on all sides. The hovercraft's headlights cut through the vapor—the light has a thickness that disappears into a wall of obscurity in the distance. The flashing lights in pursuit are stifled and look more like colored points in the rearview mirror than intimidating bright lights.

The ground level is lit up by streetlights, the tendrils of their bright white glow reaching out to their immediate vicinity. The Operator races along the street, urging every drop of speed from the freighter. He turns left once, then again, before coming to a stop on the ground next to a building and cutting the lights, hoping the police cruisers lose his scent. Colored lights appear in the passenger-side rearview mirror, the first one racing by, and the next two at a measured pace. All three pass by the dark road he's on. The fourth, traveling much slower than the others, stops at the intersection behind the freighter and inspects both sides with an ultra-bright spotlight.

"Unlucky," the Operator says.

"What?" Gabi asks.

The Operator points to the mirror on her side of the vehicle. "Watch."

The spotlight illuminates the far side before turning to the side where the Operator landed on the ground. It looks left and right in the space above the grounded craft, as if searching for an idling vehicle. Then it drops to the ground and rests on the freighter. The cruiser turns into the alley and approaches.

The industrial vehicle roars back to life and races away, moving forward and vertical at the same time. The Operator banks another left, then a right, back onto the well-lit street. The cruiser stays on his tail, its superior handling and speed capabilities handling the weak evasion attempt.

A flash of fire on the ground ahead surges forward and flies past the Operator. It collides with the cruiser, and the police vehicle erupts in a ball of flames before crashing down to the earth. Through his side mirrors, the Operator sees the other three cruisers, farther back, stop on a dime. They turn vertical, exposing their undersides while traveling back above the reclaimers.

The Operator looks where the rocket originated. There are two men and a young woman there, the two men holding rocket launchers. As he drives by, the Operator and one of the men lock eyes.

It's the burly man and the money collector who ran the race, along with the girl responsible for countdowns, protecting their illegal operation from the prying eyes of the authorities above the reclaimers. The burly man's eyes grow wide when he recognizes the Operator driving the freighter as the man who shot them the last time he was in the area.

The Operator veers into a side street just as the rocket launchers turn on him. A rocket shoots forth in a burst of flame and hits the building just behind the Operator's vehicle, covering the freighter's rear with shattered glass and concrete.

CHAPTER SEVEN

"IF YOU'RE JUST GOING to put me somewhere else, what was the point of taking me away from the orphanage?" Gabi says.

The Operator sighs. "They were using you as bait."

The two of them are sitting at the bar in the pool hall. Miguel's in the back, making breakfast. Gabi's legs dangle from the seat, since they don't reach the chair's attached bar, and every so often she kicks the wooden paneling in front of her.

"Why can't I stay here? I'll help Miguel," she says.

"Because he can't teach you everything you need to know," Miguel says, emerging from the back with three steaming bowls. Inside is a pale, sweet mush—their usual breakfast.

Chef Miguel hands out the bowls and spoons from behind the bar. Together, the three of them eat.

"The orphanage was teaching me," Gabi says, tilting her spoon to the side and watching the mush drip off and plop back down into the bowl.

The Operator sets his spoon down in his bowl. The mush is thick enough that the spoon doesn't slide. "You can't go back there."

Gabi stares at him with her lips squeezed together. "I don't want to," she mutters.

"All right then, eat."

Gabi looks at Miguel, who shrugs.

"Can you show me my mom before we leave?"

The Operator chokes on his bite. When Miguel and Gabi look at him, he says it was too hot. "That's not a good idea," he says. The only times he saw the doctor—Gabi's mother—were when he was in a dungeon below Suerte, held by Bacas, and she was in charge of keeping him alive so they could continue torturing him.

"Miguel showed me his memories of when the pool hall first opened," Gabi says into her bowl before ripping another bite off her spoon. She holds the utensil like a shovel in her fist, with her thumb over the handle.

Miguel opens his eyes wide with his lips squeezed together. "I've got to use this memory mirror sometime. If not, it just sits here!"

"You should tell him to use it sometime. Maybe he'll remember a time he was actually in a good mood," Gabi says to Miguel, gesturing towards the Operator. She shares a smile with the old man.

The Operator thinks back to the times he saw the doctor. He holds his hand out to Miguel, annoyed. Miguel reaches into the antique cash drawer, pulls out a thimble, and hands it to the Operator. The Operator puts it on his index finger and holds it up to his temple.

A woman's face appears on the mirror behind Miguel. Her hair's tied back, and her kind, tired eyes take up the entire mirror—what the Operator saw while she wrapped his head after the interrogation. When she's done, she squeezes his shoulder before helping him lie down. The Operator pulls his finger away from his head before any more memories appear; in particular, the one when she holds off his pursuers while he gets away.

"I don't have any pictures of her," Gabi says, staring down into her bowl. She sets her spoon down and walks into the back.

"At least she'll have the memory of her mother's last days," Miguel says.

The Operator shrugs, then returns to his breakfast.

After breakfast, the Operator yells to Gabi that it's time to leave. To his surprise, Miguel insists on coming along. "Traveling with you is safer than sitting in here all day. What if those kids show up again?" he says.

"What, so you're never going to open again?"

"Not with you outside the city."

"Outside the city?" Gabi says, standing in the doorway.

The Operator stares at Miguel. Miguel sucks air through his teeth, apologizing with his eyes.

"We're going to the badlands," the Operator says. "Let's go."

"I don't want to leave the city!" Gabi protests.

"Look, there are people in the badlands who can take care of you. Trust me, this is the best place for you."

"Adults always act like they know best," Gabi says, shaking her head. When everyone's ready for the trip, she follows the Operator out to the freighter sitting next to the skeleton of his former vehicle and climbs into the passenger seat. Miguel locks the pool hall's front door and climbs into her side, sharing the seat with her.

The Operator takes the same route out of the city that he took when he came in from the badlands with Fenix, the dog Bacas killed. Soon, they are weaving in and out of the rusted carcasses of abandoned vehicles on the highway. Miguel stares out the window, fascinated with looking into the distance. Gabi has her eyes on her hands in her lap.

He turns off the main road once the city disappears in the

rearview mirror, heading towards the mountains in the distance. The Sect's hideout sits in the shadow of the largest one.

The Sect is a community hell-bent on living off the land. Their founder, Druid, located a natural spring and created his home in a nearby cave decades ago. Over time, the city's outcasts, looking for another way of life, joined him. They built the community into the form the Operator found when he left the city years ago.

The members live a serene life, with all conflict resolved by Druid. He's taught them all the hand-to-hand combat of his ancestors—he claims the continued teaching is the reason he left the city in the first place. "Nobody can afford spending the time it takes to get good when the city bombards the senses all hours of the day," he said when explaining his purpose to the Operator.

Children pick up the way of life easier than the adults. They are the lifeblood of the Sect, their young minds sponging up information without years of experience in hardscrabble city life. Most arrive holding on to their parent's hand after days of travel, but some were born there. The adults find life in the Sect more difficult. Those that can't abandon their confrontational ways find themselves ostracized from the community—they often leave in the middle of the night and are never heard from again.

The Operator encountered a different challenge. He didn't mind the way of life—he even enjoyed it—but he could never grasp the nuance of the hand-to-hand combat Druid spent hours trying to teach him. To the Operator, it was a waste of time. He could never shake the sense that defending himself, or confronting another, was easier with a gun in his hand. He never outright shared these feelings with Druid, but the old man knew what was in his heart.

"There will come a time when guns won't solve your problems," Druid had said after one of the Operator's most intense episodes of frustration, when he couldn't master a front kick.

The Operator had nodded, and tried taking the sentiment to heart, but his instincts were rooted too deep. On the night he left, he gathered his belongings—which included his gun and holster—while Druid stood in his doorway.

"You'll understand why I asked you to go back when the time comes," Druid had said. Before the Operator had left, Druid told him where to spend the night. That turned out to be the night he met Fenix.

In the freighter, the Operator looks at Gabi, now certain he understands why Druid sent him back into the city.

The Operator drives all day, and the space occupied by the mountains on the horizon increases. After passing a series of rocks he remembers, he looks at the passengers with him; both Miguel and Gabi are fast asleep. Without a second thought, the Operator turns the wheel, away from the direction of the Sect.

The ground is rocky, but their ride is smooth, since the hovercraft rides atop a bed of air. They approach a large outcropping of rocks, alone in the middle of the desert. When they arrive, the Operator leaves the engine running and gets out. He climbs up the side facing the direction of the city and locates the rocky overhang where Fenix approached his fire. He chuckles to himself, remembering how skittish the dog was the first time they met. The fire's remains on the rock transports him through time, and he remembers the nights they shared together, before they found the hovercraft, walking through the desert, huddling together for warmth at night, his dog breath.

The Operator picks up a rock and, after finding a smooth spot on the wall, carves a large *F* on the surface. He steps back, decides it isn't prominent enough, then takes a piece of charcoal and colors it black.

"I shouldn't have brought you with me," the Operator says, choking up.

"He was there for you, no matter what," Miguel says.

The Operator turns around, startled. He wipes his eyes with the back of his hand.

"The girl's still asleep," Miguel says. He walks forward, putting a hand on the Operator's shoulder, and the two of them turn around and look at the marking.

"He was a good dog," Miguel says.

The Operator nods. After a moment, he breaks the silence and tells Miguel they should go. "It'll be dark soon," he says, his voice too deep, his eyes on the sky.

Miguel puts his arm around the Operator as they walk back down to the hovercraft. The Operator relaxes his shoulder and twists away. Side by side, they return to the hovercraft, and find it empty.

CHAPTER EIGHT

"Gabi!" Miguel calls out at the top of his lungs. He's walking away from the vehicle, in the direction of the city, his eyes scanning left and right. "Come back, we're running out of daylight!"

The Operator kneels down and inspects the area past the hovercraft's rear. Outside the radius of blown-away dust, he finds a small set of footprints heading off into the distance. He starts walking, following them.

Miguel, seeing the Operator's direction, follows the same trajectory, maintaining the distance between them. The mountains are on their right, and the field of boulders lies ahead. The Operator shudders—a girl raised in the city has no idea what dangers nature presents. Can she last the night if they can't find her? If she falls, or becomes trapped . . . the Operator starts second-guessing his decision to bring her into the badlands in the first place.

The Operator and Miguel begin climbing over rocks, each of them keeping tabs on the other. Twice, a shuffling rock makes the Operator stumble, and he stays upright by extending both arms onto nearby boulders, wedging himself in place. Miguel, more cautious with every step, starts lagging behind.

The shadows lengthen as they get deeper into the boulders. The Operator can still see Miguel when he turns around, but his friend's pace has slowed to a crawl. One more push before they have no choice but to turn around. Maybe she's back at the hovercraft, having lost her nerve?

The Operator finds the tallest boulder in his vicinity, climbs it, and looks around. There are rocks everywhere, and no discernible movement. He looks in every direction. There's nothing but the sound of dust particles blowing against the rocks.

He looks in the direction of where he last saw Miguel and finds nothing but more boulders. Worried something happened to him, and not wanting to lose both travelers under his watch, the Operator turns around and goes back to where he last saw Miguel. He climbs over a large rock and sees a flash of his friend's black hair. The Operator rushes over and finds Miguel standing still, a rattlesnake coiled near his leg. In front of him, in a space hidden by boulders on all sides, is Gabi. She's frozen on the ground, clutching her knees at her chest, her eyes wide open as a second snake's tongue flicks near her cheek.

Without a second thought, the Operator draws his blaster and fires a shot right next to Gabi, blowing the snake's head clean off. The headless body falls to the ground, coiling and uncoiling in the dust. With a second shot, the Operator kills the snake near Miguel in mid-lunge. The snake's head, separated from the body, clamps down on Miguel's leg, and its body writhes on the ground, the dust caking on the now-exposed end.

"Are you okay?" the Operator asks Gabi.

The scared girl stands up. Her eyes are puffy, with streaks running through the dust on her cheeks.

"I think so," Miguel and Gabi say at the same time.

Miguel reaches down and pulls the snake's head off his pants, ripping them in the process.

"He missed me," he says, looking at the Operator with a smile.

Miguel lifts Gabi up, then the Operator helps him out of the space.

"Don't run off again," the Operator says to Gabi.

"But we're happy you're safe," Miguel adds.

Gabi doesn't say a word until they're back inside the hovercraft. Then, when she's sitting next to Miguel and the Operator resumes their journey, she says, "Thanks for killing the snake."

The Operator grunts without taking his eyes off the mountain ahead. Miguel taps her leg twice and smiles.

Three orange lights appear on the mountain as the last rays of sunlight disappear over the landscape: one large, with a smaller one on each side. As the Operator and his group get closer, it becomes obvious they are torches. By the time the freighter gets beneath them, the sun has gone down and darkness envelops the desert behind them. The Operator turns off the hovercraft in a space where the flat land infiltrates into the mountain—the three fires are on the slopes that surround the space's three sides, casting light down on the travelers.

"What now?" Miguel asks.

"We get out," the Operator says.

The Operator shows them a space between the walls, hidden by the overlap of the right wall over the rear. They shuffle through and emerge into a small village surrounding a pool of water, the village surrounded on all sides by rock walls. A well-worn stone walkway runs next to the pond.

"Hardly anyone lives in the houses," the Operator explains. "They are mostly for food storage and preparation. Everyone sleeps in the caves," he says, pointing to the mountain walls surrounding the oasis.

"Where is everyone?" Gabi asks. She's in awe, and has forgotten her reluctance.

"You'll see."

The Operator leads his group along the stone path to the far wall. Beyond the last building, they find a flat expanse with a long table covered with food, each seat around it filled except four. There are over thirty people, everyone wearing a white robe with a brown belt around their waist, with plenty of children, teenagers, and young adults. A woman, with frazzled hair but smiling, sets a large plate of roast meat into the final open space in the middle of the table.

"Just in time," an older man, seated at the end of the table, says. With his hair pulled back into a ponytail and his long, slender limbs, he could pass as male or female at first glance. His deep voice betrays him.

"Of course we were right on time," the Operator says, shaking his head. "Some things never change."

"I hope you're wrong, or else I'll be hungry for the rest of my life!" Druid says, smiling. The rest of the table take that as a sign to begin filling their plates.

Everyone at the table eats their fill. Miguel groans when the chef brings out a large cake. When she looks hurt, he flashes her a smile then helps himself to a slice and wolfs it down.

Every member of the community, regardless of age, helps clear the table, leaving Druid with the Operator, Gabi, and Miguel.

"How long are you staying?" Druid asks the Operator.

"We're staying the night," the Operator says, pointing with his thumb to himself and Miguel over Gabi's head. "I need to talk to you about her staying here."

"I know, and yes," Druid says. A wave of sadness passes across his face before he returns from his daydream, looks at Gabi, and smiles. "Welcome."

"I never wanted to leave the city," Gabi says to Druid.

"You'll be safer here," the Operator responds.

Gabi stares at him through narrowed eyes before pushing away from the table and storming off.

"Can you—" the Operator begins, turning to Miguel.

"Already on it," Miguel replies. He gets up from the table with a grunt, then follows Gabi back out towards the path through the buildings they came through.

"The three of you can stay in one of the cabins tonight, just pick an empty one," Druid says. "I'll get her set up with one of the families once you leave."

"Thanks," the Operator says. The day's events and the heavy meal have left him lethargic.

The two men sit in silence, listening to the sounds of the lapping water echoing off the rock walls and the Sect members cleaning up after dinner.

"Do you want to tell me about your new limbs?" Druid says.

The Operator looks down at his right hand. "Shoot-out with the man who held her hostage—an Enforcer in the city. His men killed her mother," the Operator says. After a moment, he adds, "Did you know?"

"Know what?" Druid asks, tilting his head while he searches the Operator's face.

"That I'm an android."

"I had my suspicions."

"You could have told me."

"Would you have believed me?"

The Operator thinks for a moment then shakes his head no. "Let me go find them and get settled for the night," he says, getting up from the table.

"You won't have to search far. I'll see you at breakfast," Druid says.

The Operator leaves, wondering what Druid meant about his search, until he finds Miguel holding Gabi's hand on the stone path right outside the space. He's not holding her in place —she's resigned to her situation.

"We're staying in one of these," the Operator says, gesturing to one of the buildings along the path. He knocks on the door of the first one on their left. They hear rustling and the door opens, showing a pregnant woman, her hands on her belly. The room behind her is spotless.

"Sorry," the Operator says. "I'm looking for an empty one."

"Check two doors down," the pregnant woman inside says.

The available cabin is a square space with a waist-high pile of blankets in the corner. The Operator hands out two each to Miguel and Gabi, one to lie on and the other for warmth, and takes two himself. He lies down in front of the door. Within minutes, Miguel's gentle snoring fills the room.

The Operator wakes up the next morning confused. It takes him a moment before he realizes he's back at the Sect and remembers the events from the prior day. He looks at Miguel, still fast asleep, then at the empty space where Gabi laid. He sits up, frantic, and notices an open window.

He rushes outside, looking for Druid, prepared for a search. The old man and Gabi are at the edge of the pond. Druid is pointing to the water's source—a fissure in the rocks. Gabi looks at the Operator with all the meanness she can muster and walks away.

"She told me something interesting this morning," Druid says when it's just him and the Operator.

"What's that?"

"She knows you're an android."

The Operator, stunned, doesn't know what to say. He replays the events of yesterday, wondering when or what betrayed him.

"It's nothing you did. She said she can always tell the difference."

"How?"

"There's a halo around androids living people don't have—she calls it a glow. She says it's obvious to her," Druid says. After a pause, he adds, "Where did you find her?"

"In an orphanage. Bacas, the Enforcer, kept her hostage so her mother would do what he wanted."

"Did Bacas know what he had on his hands?"

"I'm not sure. But if he did, he didn't tell anyone else. They wouldn't have let her go to the orphanage."

"There are powerful people in the city who would pay a lot of money for a talent like hers."

"Or do whatever it took to get their hands on her."

Druid stares into the water and releases a long exhale.

"You'll be going after breakfast?"

The Operator thinks for a moment. "No, I think we'll head back now. I'll drop him off and keep going. It's time I left the city behind for good."

Druid looks into the Operator's eyes. "One day, she'll understand all that you've done for her."

CHAPTER NINE

"I STILL DON'T KNOW why we couldn't stay for breakfast," Miguel says, climbing into the passenger side of the freighter. The evaporating moisture on the surrounding rocks creates a mist around the mountains. The torches that guided the Operator last night are now simple wooden sticks poking from the ground a short climb away.

"You had enough food last night to last you for days," the Operator replies with a laugh, turning on the vehicle. "You just wanted another chance to compliment the chef."

Miguel turns to the Operator, feigning shock. "She seemed nice, that's all!"

"Sure," the Operator says. He backs the hovercraft out of the space within the rocks, turns around, and the pair begin driving away, heading back towards the main highway leading to the city.

They travel at a relaxed pace, knowing there's nothing waiting for them back in the city. "You know, I'd never been out of the city until yesterday?" Miguel says, filling the silence.

The Operator doesn't reply.

"Not once. Everyone talks about the badlands like there's some hidden danger. It doesn't seem so bad."

"It's not, if you're with the Sect. Alone? It's miserable."

"How long were you out here before you found them?"

"A week or two—I lost track of days. But I didn't find them."

Miguel looks at the Operator, confused.

"They found me."

The Operator continues when Miguel doesn't answer. "I don't remember the hunger, but I do remember being so thirsty I couldn't think straight. I woke up one morning and Druid was there, looking down at me. There were two men with him—one stood beneath each of my arms and helped me limp back to their community."

"Couldn't even walk?"

"Not on my own. Looking back, I wonder how much it was because I *believed* I needed water to survive. If I am an android, why did it affect me so much?"

"The mind is a powerful thing, amigo."

The Operator nods. A deep part of him delights in knowing he's transcended normal human needs. "Turns out, I was right on their doorstep—I think that's why they helped me. Knowing Druid, maybe he wanted to see if I'd find the place on my own."

"He sees things, doesn't he?"

"Sees things?"

"Like the future. Possibilities."

"I never knew how much. But yes, he's never surprised by the way events unfold."

"Do you think he knew we would leave before breakfast?"

"If you don't stop thinking about food—" the Operator says, turning to Miguel.

Miguel looks at the Operator, serious, before a broad smile spreads over his face. He leans forward. "There's the rock," he says, pointing.

The Operator turns to his left, remembers his canine friend, then turns his eyes back to their path.

Miguel, still looking, remarks on the dust.

"Are there dust storms out here?"

"Sometimes."

"Looks like there's one heading towards your rock."

The Operator looks again, to the right of the landmark. The dust looks different from any dust storm he's seen before. Instead of a broad, sweeping mass, the dust he sees is a straight line.

"Looks like the dust is heading straight to the Sect," Miguel observes.

"I don't think it's a dust storm," the Operator says.

"What else could it be?" Miguel says. He's still leaning forward, watching, when he realizes the path is a direct line between the city and the Sect. "They're going after the girl!"

"They want me, not the girl," the Operator replies. "Besides, they'll never find the place."

"But what if they do?"

"Druid can handle it."

Miguel's mouth hangs open in shock.

"What about the person who the orphanage worker called? The one using Gabi as bait. You said he showed up with android security! Maybe he wants her back!"

"Look. We saved her from becoming another lost city kid, took her where she can grow. We've done our part. Besides, it's just dust."

"We both know it's not just dust."

The Operator ignores the statement. "Now, let's go back to the city, drop you off, and I can leave all this behind."

"Why did you save her if you aren't going to take every step for her to have a future?"

"It's not my problem. I did my part."

"It is your problem!" Miguel opens the passenger-side door. "Either turn around and go back or I'm going back without you."

The Operator looks at Miguel, measuring his intent, before turning around. "If it's just a bunch of dust—"

"Then we can turn around and go back, and you can leave all this behind you, like you keep saying."

The Operator doesn't head towards the Sect, aware that in the event they are going for him, or Gabi, arriving at the same time as the pursuers wouldn't turn out well for him. Instead, he goes towards the rock formation where he met Fenix. He arrives well after the procession of dust has passed, and in the distance, between himself and the Sect, are a fleet of vehicles.

"They're going for her," Miguel says.

"Or for me," the Operator adds. "Well, we're in it this far . . ." he says with a shrug.

The Operator doesn't go towards the Sect—he aims for a spot on the right, far from the main entrance, hoping nobody ahead of him sees the dust his vehicle kicks up cutting a line behind them.

"Where are we going?" Miguel asks.

"There's another way in," the Operator says.

There's a pass at the spot where the freighter reaches the mountains. They drive uphill for a time before the Operator parks the vehicle. They both jump out.

"Follow me," the Operator says. The sun is bright overhead as the pair weave between, jump over, and climb up the boulders in their path. The Operator leads with certainty until they are at the uppermost ridge over the opening in the mountain where the community sits. They look down on the pond.

The man with the glasses stands on one side, his hands behind his back, watching his minions gather everyone they can find. There aren't many. Among the captured are Druid, the chef, and the pregnant woman in the hut. Plus some younger members of the Sect who helped in the kitchen during dinner the night before.

"Why don't they fight back? You said they're expert fighters," Miguel says.

"Part of Druid's whole thing is knowing when the time is right. Never made sense to me until the showdown with Bacas." Druid's the best there is, but even he can't dodge gunfire.

"Stay here," the Operator whispers to Miguel. Then, he crawls down between the rocks. He suspects the man in glasses sent sentinels into the rocks surrounding the village, and he carries a fist-sized rock in his hand, ready for stealthy incapacitation. He's surprised when he doesn't find any.

He arrives at a large cave. Inside, just beyond the daylight, are seven security androids lying inert. The Operator walks forward, his hands up, and a member of the Sect emerges from behind a rock. Then, dozens more leave their hiding places, appearing before the Operator.

"Are you going to shoot them?" one of the younger Sect members asks.

"Where's Gabi?" the Operator says.

"She's here," one of the adults says. She pushes Gabi forward. "We've got to go," the Operator says to the girl.

Without protesting, she stands by his side with her head down.

"They want us. They'll leave the Sect alone if we leave," the Operator tells the Sect members. "Tell Druid I'll take her back into the city."

A resigned Gabi follows when the Operator pulls on her arm.

Outside the cave, the Operator hides behind a rock and looks down at the infiltrators and the captives. The man with the glasses is pacing in front of Druid.

"I won't ask you again: we know she's here. Tell us where you hid her!" His voice is crystal clear, amplified even at this distance by the funneling rocks.

Druid bows his head. "It has to be this way," his booming voice says. The Operator knows he's talking to him.

"It's true, the girl was here. She's . . . special," Druid says, talking now to the man in glasses.

"Special? Bacas held her captive to keep her mother in line."

"If I tell you, will you leave us in peace?" Druid asks.

"I don't care about your little community, I want the girl. And right now, I want to know why she's so special, why Bacas held her hostage for so long."

Druid sighs. "She can sense androids."

Gabi looks at the Operator, embarrassed that her secret is out in the world. And his. The Operator shrugs. "I couldn't hide it forever," he says.

"She was taken back to the city this morning," Druid continues. "In a white freighter—"

"Yes, we know all about how she escaped the orphanage and got here. The man responsible used his identification getting into the upper levels."

"If you leave now, you can catch them," Druid says.

The man in glasses looks at Druid. "If I find out you helped them . . ."

"I found out he was running from the law this morning and asked him to leave. We've done nothing."

The man in glasses looks at the security forces he's brought with him. "Burn them to the ground," he says, gesturing to the village's buildings while walking back towards the hidden entrance.

The last thing the Operator sees is the captives taken to the edge of the pond and their wooden buildings put to the torch.

He turns and leaves with Gabi, meets back up with Miguel, and together they go back to the waiting hovercraft.

They continue through the pass and spend the rest of the day on the far side of the mountains, separated from the city. As night falls, they make their way back, traveling slowly enough that the Operator can dodge the rusted-out cars littering the highway in darkness while the neon lights covering the city's buildings beckon to them from ahead.

CHAPTER TEN

THE POOL HALL'S front door hangs twisted from the top hinge —both the Operator and Miguel notice it from afar during their approach. Miguel's head tilts back against the headrest, his eyes closed in frustration.

"Stay in here," the Operator says to Gabi when their hovercraft touches back down to earth. He gets out, his blaster drawn.

Miguel steps down from the passenger side and follows the Operator to the entrance, using him for protection. They both peer in. The few overhead lights still functioning are flickering, feeble attempts at fulfilling their purpose. Broken glass from shattered lights litters the ground. The pool tables are scratched, cue sticks broken, and colorful fragments sit amid white billiard ball dust.

"Bet those kids came back," Miguel says.

The Operator nods in agreement. "Stay here." He steps inside, scanning the room for traces of movement. The few bottles of Serum Miguel kept on hand are shattered, with glass and liquid on the bar and floor from where they were struck against the corner. Cracks spider out from the holes in the memory mirror. There is as much destruction as possible, except for the barstools—those were left alone.

After checking the back, the Operator walks back to the front door. "Nobody's here," he tells Miguel. He looks into the hovercraft. "You can get out," he says to Gabi, beckoning with his hand.

The three travelers go inside. Miguel takes a big breath, followed by a long, slow exhale through puffed cheeks. Gabi stares at the shattered memory mirror like she's lost all hope of seeing her mom ever again.

"There's a broom in the back," Miguel says, clapping his hands and nodding. He inspects the wasted Serum as he walks past the bar, disappears in the back, then returns with a broom in hand. "They didn't bother anything back there," he reports.

"They were too busy out here," the Operator says.

Gabi still hasn't moved. Miguel puts a hand on her shoulder and tells her to go into the back. "We'll take care of this," he says.

The Operator picks up the larger pieces of destruction while Miguel sweeps up broken glass. "We just got this place fixed up again too," Miguel says, shaking his head. "Back to square one."

Later that night, Miguel and Gabi sleep while the Operator stands guard. It's his turn to sleep when Miguel wakes up in the early morning, and after a few hours of rest he wakes up to the smell of breakfast.

"Eat," Miguel says when the Operator walks into the pool hall's main room. He's sitting down next to Gabi at the bar with empty bowls in front of them.

The Operator wolfs down his room-temperature food before telling Miguel he's going to talk to the White Jackets.

"I'll be back later. You two, stay in the back."

"There's more work to do out here," Miguel says.

"And what if those kids come back?"

"What are they going to do? They've already destroyed everything!"

"At least keep the blaster we took from the kid ready, for protection," the Operator says. When he leaves, he moves the freighter and parks it so that it's blocking the front door.

Gamma district is split in two by the ancient railway that the city's residents used before the vertical revolution. The split was the line that separated two gangs before the Operator killed Bacas, the chief Enforcer and leader of one of the groups; his authority was granted by the government. Their rival gang, the White Jackets, were tolerated because they manufactured the best Serum in the city, and Bacas could keep the government-provided Stim for himself as long as their product flowed. The White Jackets took over both sides of Gamma when Bacas disappeared, and without a replacement assigned by the higher levels, they've been in charge ever since.

Gamma's market is beneath a patchwork series of tarps close to the rail line. One of the first things the White Jackets did was rebuild a bridge over the rails, providing access to the market for everyone within Gamma. The resulting economic prosperity cemented their place within the hearts of people on both sides of the midline. The Operator walks among the crowd between the stalls of various food vendors, looking for the white jacket indicative of one of the gang's members. Besides the gang's trademark article of clothing, people below the reclaimers don't have the same attachment to dress as those who live higher up. Both men and women on the surface wear dark-colored, rough-cut cloth garments, with the occasional splash of color—the Operator fits right in with his black outfit accented with silver.

When he doesn't find a white jacket along his initial route, the Operator turns down the street towards the abandoned train station. The market extends down this street as well—a new expansion—with vendors selling everything from jewelry to furniture. There isn't a white jacket in sight. He continues down the row of merchants until he passes a furniture shop and checks if they have anything the destroyed pool hall could use.

A short man with gray hair ringing his bald head jumps down from a high stool when the Operator approaches. "Are you looking for anything in particular?" he says, his sweet voice rising and falling.

"Just seeing what you have." There's an ancient bed frame, various-sized lamps, and padded chairs. The Operator is about to leave when he spots an old cash register, the same as the one in the pool hall. He doesn't remember seeing one in the destroyed pool hall after returning from the badlands.

"Oh, you have good taste!" the merchant says.

The Operator opens the cash register and finds the thimble for the memory mirror. He takes it, and pockets it, without the seller noticing. "When did you get this?" he says, patting the machine.

"Brand new, came in last night!"

"And who sold it to you?"

The merchant scrambles for words. "We do business with many people. It's impossible to remember."

The Operator pulls out his blaster and shoots one of the lamps. Broken glass and porcelain fall to the ground.

"A young man brought it in yesterday, late, after I closed for the night," the merchant stammers.

"What did he look like?"

"Like a normal guy? How should I know?"

The Operator points his blaster at the man. "You better remember soon."

"He's coming back soon! I told him I'd keep it here and pay him for it today."

The Operator nods. "I'll be right across the aisle. Point him out when he gets here." He looks around and settles his gaze on one of the merchant's lamps. "Turn this on and off," he says, pointing to it. He leaves the merchant alone and sits inside a nearby store, unbothered because the man selling chairs witnessed his neighbor's harassment.

He doesn't wait long. The same young man who watched the Operator deal with his two friends in the pool hall strolls into the furniture shop with his head held high. The stammering merchant turns the light on and off three times before the young man points out the behavior, shaking his head. The lamp stays off.

The Operator watches the young man put a finger in the merchant's face before storming off. He gets up and follows the thief back through the market's center, to a stall at the very end of the far side. There, the man goes into a smoking lounge, then through curtains in the back. The Operator walks past sluggish men lost in deep cushions before going through the curtains himself.

Once through, he's struck in the back with a metal bar.

He stumbles forward, catching himself against a stout pillar holding up the canopy overhead. A swift strike lands on his right side, leaving him bent sideways in pain, wheezing. On a second strike to his side, he catches the bar, twisting it away from his attacker.

The man kicks the Operator in the back of the knee, forcing him to kneel. Then, he kicks him in the back, sending him sprawling on the ground.

"Get up," the young man says, bouncing side to side on the balls of his feet.

The Operator stands, his blaster drawn.

The young man raises his hands. "You shoot me, every White Jacket in the area will come for your head."

The Operator, his elbow pinned to his side, tilts his head. *"You're a White Jacket?"*

"Why so surprised? Is it because I'm not wearing one?"

The Operator nods. "Yes, to be honest."

"Nobody wears those stupid things. No reason to put a target on our backs—no telling when the government will send down a new Enforcer."

"Take me to Klepsydra," the Operator says.

It's the young man's turn to be surprised. "You know her name?"

The Operator shoots the wall next to the young man's head. "Next time, I won't miss."

"Okay, okay. I should have hit you in the head," he mutters.

Instead of walking back out through the smoking lounge, the young man leads the Operator up a staircase behind the establishment. They travel up a level, go farther away from the market, then cross over a walkway to another building. Then, they go up once more and walk into an abandoned theater.

A table in the middle of the stage has a large, ornate chair at the head on the left, with multiple smaller chairs around the rest of it. Klepsydra, the leader of the White Jackets after her sister, Iris, was killed, sits in the privileged position. Her hair is different, longer now, but the bird tattoo on her neck is still the same. Everyone present has on a tight-fitting, white bomber-style jacket.

Everyone at the table turns and watches the Operator approach the stage behind the young man through the descending rows of chairs. When they realize one of their own is held hostage, everyone but Klepsydra withdraws their weapon and points it at the pair.

"What are you doing here?" Klepsydra snaps.

"Sorry, ma'am, he made me—"

"Not you. Him."

The young man stops walking, turns around, and looks at the Operator. The blaster poke in his back reminds him to keep walking.

"I need your help," the Operator says.

Klepsydra laughs. The rest of the table join her when they realize. "With what?" she says with disdain.

"Protection. I've got a girl being chased by the upper levels."

"And how'd you find this one?" Klepsydra says, nodding towards the hostage. She looks at the rest of her table. "He's one of ours, right?"

The young man's shoulders sag, and he drops his head.

"He is, maintains order in the market," an old crone on Klepsydra's left tells her.

"How can you maintain order when you get caught by him?" Klepsydra says, addressing the young man.

"He followed me. I wasn't paying attention," he says to the ground, loud enough for the questioner to hear.

"I followed him because he trashed the pool hall," the Operator says.

"And what, you want me to fix it?"

"No, I just want help with protection. Against whoever's hunting the girl."

Klepsydra looks at the young man and lifts her chin. The Operator pulls his blaster away then kicks him forward. He stumbles and falls, then stays on his knees.

"Why should we help you?"

"I killed Bacas so you could take this side of the midline," the Operator says.

The young man turns around, his mouth open in shock.

"You weren't doing us a favor. You were repaying a debt. We're even."

"I just need help dealing with whoever's after the girl. What's it going to take?"

Klepsydra leans forward and puts her elbows on the table, a wicked smile pasted on her face. "You have to kill your friends in the midline."

CHAPTER ELEVEN

"THE MIDLINERS ARE KILLING our messengers. To them, every rat is food," Klepsydra explains, disgusted. "We've tried sending the rats with threatening notes—it doesn't work. Then, they killed my nephew when I sent him down there to talk with them."

The rest of the table murmurs in agreement.

"I don't know if they can read," the Operator says.

"Doesn't matter!" Klepsydra says, raising her voice. Her eyes narrow. "They killed one of ours, and they have to pay."

"I'll go talk to them," the Operator says, holstering his weapon. After he says goodbye to the council, the former hostage leads him back down to the market. The Operator leaves him behind and walks towards the abandoned station on his way to the midliners, making sure he gives the merchant who sells stolen goods a cold stare.

The midliners are humans who have become deformed from growing up drinking tainted water. When the reclaimers are full, the toxins the system withdraws from the air gather and appear in the environment as acid rain. This trickles down belowground, to the abandoned rail and sewer system where the midliners live. The Operator spent time belowground, recovering after being tortured, with the aid of a midliner named Usryd.

The abandoned train station has changed since the Operator last visited. It was the only spot where the White Jackets and Bacas's team of Enforcers ever met, the lone point in the entirety of Gamma district where their territories touched. Nobody used the station for fear of death while the two gangs were locked in struggle—his own visit caused a stir and almost got him killed. Now, since it isn't separating two gangs anymore, the station is covered in trash. Rats scurry along the platform, both the smaller, wild variety and the larger, well-fed messenger type with attached harnesses. There were rats in the station before, but never this many, and never the messengers.

The Operator jumps down onto the tracks and walks into the darkness beyond the lit station. He was walking in the opposite direction the last time he was here, heading towards the light for his final confrontation with Bacas and the rest of his gang. There are two kinds of shadows in the tunnel: the open spaces and the darker pillars supporting the rest of the city above. Every so often he gets the sensation he's being watched. No surprise; the midliner men spend most of the day out hunting rats—there has to be one that spots him.

All of a sudden, a rock hits him in the chest. "Get out," a reedy voice says from the shadows in front of him.

"I'm coming to speak with Usryd."

There's a shuffle in the shadows ahead and the Operator can make out a humanoid shape walking on all fours. "Usryd's my brother," the midliner says. A moment later, he asks, "How do you know him?"

"He helped me get my sight back."

"Oh, it's you!" the midliner exclaims. "Thank god you're here. Follow me."

The midliner leads the Operator deeper into the abandoned rails. They take a number of twists and turns, going through tunnels for trains and human-sized walkways. The camp they arrive at is in another abandoned train station, its entrance collapsed and inaccessible to the outside world—the same one where the Operator practiced shooting after Bacas's blows to the head had ruined his sight.

The sole light fixture is on, but covered. There's a group of midliners beneath the diminished artificial light, and many more congregated around a fire on the opposite platform. The two sources provide plenty of light when compared to the darkness in the tunnels. The targets the Operator practiced shooting with are both still set up.

Usryd recognizes the Operator right away. "You've come back!" he says, rushing forward and grabbing his hand when the Operator climbs onto the platform. His excitement is short-lived; he becomes serious right after leading the Operator to his pile of rags.

"We've got a problem," Usryd tells the Operator, sitting down in a full squat. The Operator sits down cross-legged. Usryd pushes his long, stringy hair out of his face, putting his pale, green-tinged skin on full display. "One of the surface-dwellers is dead."

"I've heard."

Usryd leans forward, putting both hands on the ground. "So they know about it! Are they coming for us?"

"They sent me."

Usryd sits back. "It was Aldor," he says, with a nod towards the rails. His brother is sitting near the edge of the platform. "The man got angry when he was told to go back, started shooting into the dark. Aldor kept throwing rocks at him—one hit him in the head. He fell and never got up."

The Operator looks around the platform. There's evidence

of wild shooting on the far side of the platform they're seated on, small dark holes in the wall and floor among the shadows. "You took their gun," he says.

"I've been practicing, like you taught me," Usryd says. He looks at the ground. "I'm not very good."

"It gets easier with time," the Operator says. "The man you killed was related to their leader."

Aldor rushes forward and sits down near Usryd. "It was an accident!"

"I know, but they're not happy about it. And they're also not happy they're losing their messenger rats."

Usryd pulls his head back in disgust. "How are we supposed to tell? They're rats, in the tunnels." A mischievous glint appears in his eye. "They are fatter though," he adds.

"Why wasn't this a problem before?" the Operator asks.

"More of their rats are coming down below the surface now because they throw their trash down the sewers," Usryd explains.

"Instead of letting it pile on the streets . . ." the Operator says, thinking out loud. "The market on the surface has expanded, and they need all the room they can get."

"And their rats now come down here, chasing the trash. It's been great for us," Usryd says, smiling.

"You need to stop killing the messengers," the Operator says. "The people who use them will come down and kill you if you don't."

"How can I stop people from eating?" Usryd asks. "I'm only one man!"

The Operator takes a deep breath.

"What if we stop the rats from coming down in the first place?" Aldor says.

"Lower your voice," Usryd hisses, his eyes shuffling to the

midliners around them. They aren't paying attention. Or, they don't seem like they are.

"Well, if they don't come down here, we can't kill them," Aldor whispers.

"How can we block the sewers? They're high up," Usryd says.

"If they're high off the ground, how do the rats get down to the trash?" the Operator asks.

"Never underestimate a rat chasing food," Aldor says. "They find ways."

"So, we block off these sewers, there's no trash and no reason for the rats to come down. Is there one nearby?"

"There are eight new piles of trash. The largest is a short walk away."

Usryd, Aldor, and the Operator walk through the darkness, past the main rail line, to the closest sewer access point. They kick trash and rats to the side as they approach. The Operator wades through a waist-deep pile of debris, old food, and junk until he stands beneath the circular shaft that leads to the surface. Thin rays of light filter down through the handholds on the manhole cover, illuminating the ladder made of thin metal bars attached to one side of the shaft. The ceiling, and the bottom rung, is too high for any of them to reach.

The Operator looks into the surrounding shadows, his eyes making out shapes now that he's accustomed to the low light. There's a long, heavy beam nearby. He grabs it and leans it on a nearby pillar. Stepping back, he runs up the angled surface and launches himself towards the shaft, getting a grip on the bottom rung at the apex of his jump. After getting a grip with both hands, he climbs up and inspects the cover. There's a metal hook underneath, and two holes on the perimeter. He descends, then drops back down to the ground, landing in the trash pile.

"We need a long, thin piece of metal," the Operator says.

Usryd and Aldor scurry away, each bringing back a viable option. "Just one," the Operator says, taking Aldor's. He steps on one end, bending it, then steps on it again, making a right-angled hook. "Pass this to me when I'm up there," he says.

The two brothers nod, not realizing the Operator's eyes aren't as sensitive as theirs. He assumes they understand despite their unseen confirmation and he launches himself back up to the shaft's ladder.

"Okay, pass it up. Hook side first," the Operator says when he's secured himself by pushing his back against the wall behind him while the ladder supports his feet. He reaches down, finds the hook, and feeds it through the space between the ladder and the wall, bringing the hook with him as he ascends.

At the top, near the manhole cover, the Operator pulls on the hook with all his weight, bending it just enough so it can pass outside the ladder while the rest of its length is still between the rungs and the wall. As more of the metal emerges from behind the ladder, it's easier to bend, and the Operator does so until he can hook it onto the bottom of the manhole cover. Then, he drops down until he comes to the end of the thin piece of metal, bending it against the metal rungs of the ladder, sealing the sewer shut.

"Nobody's lifting that thing up anymore," the Operator says, dusting his hands on his pants. He picks up the metal beam from the ground, balancing it on one shoulder. "Let's get the rest of these other guys closed off too."

The Operator, with the help of Usryd and Aldor, closes all eight covers using the same method. All the trash piles beneath the shafts are smaller than the first, and the rats present scatter when they arrive. "They won't get trapped down here?" the Operator asks.

Usryd laughs. "There are other ways for them to get out."

Aldor, also laughing, says, "The rats didn't use the ladders to come down, why should they need them to go back up? Rats come and go as they please."

Usryd and Aldor walk the Operator back to the tunnel's exit. A messenger rat passes by their feet, scurrying in the darkness. "Try and tell them not to kill the large ones, until they all go back to the surface," the Operator says. He holds up a hand before Usryd can protest. "I know that you're only one man, but try. Tell them people will come kill them."

The well-lit train station is visible from the shadows. "What about that trash?" Aldor says, pointing to the platform. "Their rats come into the tunnels because of that."

"We'll leave it for a bit, lure the rats in the tunnels out, then clean it up," the Operator says, as if it's his decision to make.

CHAPTER TWELVE

Two MEN STAND guard outside the pool hall; the freighter outside has been moved. There are two large puncture holes on its side and scrape marks on the concrete leading away from where it sat before. The Operator spots the situation from down the block—he's on his way back to talk to Miguel about the stolen cash register and see if the pool hall owner wants it back. Fearing the worst for his friend and Gabi, the Operator darts into a side street and runs behind the building before the guards see him.

The pool hall's back door is ajar. The Operator pulls out his blaster. During his approach, the Operator peeks under the lid of the dumpster in the alley behind the pool hall, in case Miguel and Gabi are hidden inside. A messenger rat scurries out a rusted hole in the side—it's otherwise empty. When the Operator gets to the rear entrance, he pulls the door open with his left hand, his weapon ready in his right. The entranceway is empty. He walks in and hears shuffling in the main room.

The back hallway, home to the one-wall kitchen, runs perpendicular to the back door's entranceway. The pool hall's main area is through an opening on the hallway's left, and at the end are doors for the storage room and bedroom. The Operator peeks around the corner—the two doors are open. He slinks against the wall until he gets to the opening to the main room, then looks at the intruders.

There are four men, three of them standing still while one paces between the pool tables. The pacing man is the man with glasses that has been chasing the Operator from the orphanage to the badlands, and now to the pool hall. He's short, with a comb-over and a thin mouth, and wears all white beneath a black trench coat. Two of the three men stand still, their eyes wide open as if they're staring into the distance. Android security, wearing matching dark gray compression suits. The third unmoving man seems alert, ready, and for the most part, normal —other than the two guns he has attached to the ends of his arms instead of hands. He also wears a black trench coat, and his long dark hair, peppered with gray, surrounds a face made for snarling.

No Miguel or Gabi in sight.

"We're not the only ones after them. Where else can they go?" the man in glasses says. His high-pitched voice doesn't match his demeanor.

Nobody answers him.

All of a sudden, the two-gunned android looks at the space leading to the back and holds both arms up in the Operator's direction.

"There's someone here," a gruff voice says.

"Check it out," the man in glasses says to the two standard security androids with a wave of his hand. They march forward, guns drawn, while their two-gunned companion stays put.

The Operator turns and runs. He bursts through the rear door. There are two androids at the end of the alley, on the side the Operator came from, and they open fire as soon as the running Operator appears. The Operator fires once, hitting one of them in the chest, before running the opposite direction in a zigzag pattern. Shots from one blaster fly past him, until the two androids emerge from the pool hall and their gunfire joins the mix.

A shot from the android at the end of the alley hits one of the two pursuers closest to the Operator, and the struck android's next shot strikes the building high above the Operator's head. The Operator turns left at the corner and continues running. There's a broken-down car left over from the ground-based travel days on the far side of the street, no more than a shadow of what it once was. Taking shelter behind it, the Operator turns, gets down on one knee, and aims his blaster where the androids should appear, using the hood of the car for support.

His pursuers turn the corner in a full sprint, one of them with a limp arm. The Operator fires three rapid shots in quick succession, and three headless bodies collapse to the ground. He stands up, looking at the three bodies, and is about to run when a large purple hoverbarge, wide and flat, descends through the haze from above. It hovers above the incapacitated androids.

The Operator wonders if the craft is for retrieval; let no resource go to waste. Instead, more than a dozen more androids jump down, landing in a kneeling stance. Each one has a blaster rifle in hand, with blaster pistols strapped to their thighs.

Then, the android with two guns for hands appears around the corner, taking long strides forward. Before any of the reinforcements stand and take aim, the two-handed android has both arms horizontal, shooting at the Operator without breaking his stride. The booming shots ring out, reverberating off the surrounding buildings—a stark contrast to the typical muffled pops of most blasters.

The Operator ducks, and the shots hit the wall right behind

where his head was a moment before. The reinforcement androids standing up between the two-gunned android and the Operator don't affect the two-gunned attacker's trajectory, or shot frequency; those in his way get mowed down. Each shot leaves a gaping hole in the struck android.

After losing several of their own, the reinforcements evacuate the space between the overpowered blasters and their target. A flurry of shots hit the ancient car the Operator hides behind, heavy thuds from booming shots and thin cracks from the blaster rifles' high-pitched whine.

Protected for a moment, the Operator looks down at his single blaster, shaking his head. There's a manhole cover next to him—the perfect avenue for escape, if he hadn't sealed it shut.

With a shrug, he leans over and looks around the edge of the car. The mass of attackers creeps forward, a high-viscosity fluid comprised of shooting androids. One of their shots pierces through the protection, disintegrating part of the wall behind the vehicle's center, opening a small hole.

Inspired, the Operator aims his blaster at the building and unleashes a torrent of shots at the wall, sending powdered stone flying. When he stops shooting, grateful his gun hasn't revolted against him like it did at the playground, the dust settles, revealing a hole the size of a barrel lid.

The Operator reaches his blaster over his head and fires wild shots in the direction of his attackers. Their shots continue, undeterred. He prepares himself with a series of rapid breaths, then scrambles forward and dives through the opening in the wall.

He doesn't project himself far enough and ends up with his thighs against the bottom of the hole, his torso leaning towards the ground, and his feet still outside, dangling in the air. With the blaster still in his hand, he pushes against the wall, forcing himself through until he collapses on the ground. The room is an old office, with fluorescent lights, bare walls, a massive wooden desk, and years of dust covering every surface. His black pants are covered in dust, and a mixture of dust and fluid coagulates on his shin where he's been shot.

Poking the wound doesn't produce any pain. He stands, walks back and forth, and still feels nothing out of the ordinary. A few test jumps reveal no issues. A blaster rifle's barrel poking through the hole pulls him back to the present—he grabs it and takes it from his pursuer before firing a handful of shots through the hole himself. When the android falls, another takes its place.

The Operator, now with his personal blaster and a rifle, sets his feet and starts firing shots with both weapons through the hole in the wall. Some of the rifle shots miss the target, since he's holding it with his left hand and has the butt pinned against his hip. When one android tries looking down the barrel of his gun through the hole, he receives a blaster shot to the face.

"This is too easy," the Operator says with a laugh. He begins seeing androids he's already shot come back for another attempt at coming through the hole. They have dark spots on their gray compression suits from leaking internal fluids. The Operator keeps a lookout for a black trench coat while he fires, hoping the two-gunned android is foolish enough to get in his line of fire.

The reinforcements pull back, leaving the space outside the hole clear. The Operator wonders how many were in front of him, and if some had split off and are now coming into the building from the back. The dust in the room floats in the air, illuminated by the flickering lights overhead. The hole the Operator jumped through has gotten bigger, both from the androids' attempts at breaching and from the Operator's shots. Outside, the flashing neon lights play against the broken-down car's skeletal surface.

A wrenching sound rings out from another part of the compromised wall—the sound of metal piercing stone. Over and over the sound rings out, filling the small room, a rhythmic pounding. It increases in speed over time, jackhammering until cracks appear in the office wall. Then, two blasts boom out from the cracks, demolishing the wall and revealing two guns attached to two arms covered by black trench coat sleeves.

CHAPTER THIRTEEN

THE OPERATOR fires two shots into the space opened up by the android with guns for hands. The attacker stumbles back but doesn't fall when both projectiles find their target. The android fires twice while off-balance, hitting the wall and widening the hole, before the Operator can fire again. When he regains his balance, he attacks the wall with a renewed fervor, going berserk in his attempts at reaching the Operator.

Amazed and without any ideas of what else could slow the overpowered android down, the Operator turns and runs. He has a loose concept of where he is in the city but has no idea where he could go. Survival is his lone concern. Running up stairs, through corridors, and across walkways, he puts as much distance as he can between himself and the androids sent after him by the man in glasses. After running down a series of corridors on the third level, he reaches a dead end. The closest door is locked. The Operator pulls his blaster from his holster and shoots the lock. A dent outlined in black appears on the door. Distant footsteps echo down the hall. Taking aim with the blaster rifle—a more powerful firearm—he then fires a series of shots into the door, making a half circle around the lock. He kicks the door, and it cracks open with a groan. The split reveals that the door is made of thick metal. Two more kicks and there's enough space for his body. He slithers through and finds himself in the middle of two long tables that run the length of the room. Wrinkled, shirtless old men sit between the table and the outside walls, leaving the space between open. Broken-down boxes sit on the ground beneath the tables, and stacks of sealed boxes line the walls. On the table are empty finger-sized vials and flasks of clear liquid.

The men stare at the Operator, the sclerae of their questioning eyes a vivid blue.

"Is this Stim?" the Operator says, forgetting his pursuers for the moment.

The man closest to the door grunts while nodding his head. Then, he raises his hand in the shape of a gun, points it at the Operator, and lifts it in a sharp motion before pointing at the intruder.

"I'll deal with them when the time comes," the Operator says.

The old man grunts and shrugs.

"Who do you all work for?" Without Bacas in charge, there's no one regulating the flow of Stim from the upper levels. The government should still be promoting productivity by sending each resident's allocation down, but as far as the Operator knows, all of Gamma district still consumes Serum, limiting their need for Stim.

The old man grunts again.

"Fine, don't tell me," the Operator says, looking behind him in sudden remembrance of his haste.

The old man shakes his head, then opens his mouth. His tongue is gone. The rest of the old men open their mouths—all of them are empty. The Operator holsters his blaster, slings the rifle over his shoulder, and runs down the length of the tables between the tongueless old men, going through the back window to the attached balcony. There's no fire escape, though there is new metal exposed where one was removed.

There's a matching balcony on the building across the alley. The Operator climbs onto the railing. A grunt from the closest man pulls his attention back into the room, where the first security android squeezes into the room. The pursuer pulls his blaster rifle up to his shoulder as the Operator jumps.

His chest hits the top of the railing on the adjacent building's third floor, his arms hanging limp over the edge. The sudden impact takes his breath away and he slips, his hands sliding over the railing and down the vertical posts. He loses contact with the third floor and falls.

One hand grabs hold of the railing on the second-story balcony, yanking him to a stop. His shoulder screams with the sudden pressure but doesn't separate. He looks back at the balcony he jumped from and finds it empty, but in the space between the two buildings he sees the transport ship that deposited the reinforcements in the first place. It's hovering just above the reclaimers, its edges blurred in the haze.

The Operator climbs up the railing and hops over, then plunges into the second floor just as a shot hits the balcony where he stood a moment before. He's in a shabby studio apartment; nobody's home. There's one sagging bed, a small refrigerator, and a sink full of dishes. Hurrying through, he looks back when he hears a loud thud. An android falls from the third floor and misses grabbing hold of the second. Another android aims at the second floor, lands on the railing with his chest, and flips backwards, falling to the ground. The Operator hopes the rest encounter the same fate but doesn't stick around to find out—he rushes out of the apartment, down the stairs, and emerges from the building across from the train station.

The market on his left is bustling. The furniture shop,

where the antique cash register sits, has a crowd of people inspecting the objects placed closest to the front. Trash is piled up between a manhole cover and the building, with deep scratch marks in the ancient asphalt where someone tried digging up the sealed opening.

The people in the market look in the Operator's direction. At first he thinks they're noticing him, and, self-conscious, he readjusts the blaster rifle on his back. He then realizes that their gaze is towards the sky. The massive hoverbarge is off in the distance, shimmering purple illuminated by the neon lights from moving billboards high above.

The Operator groans. He's about to run through the train station and lead his pursuers away from the market when the shopper closest to him points past him. Androids in gray compression, each one of them sporting dark spots of wetness from their spilled internal fluids, stagger from the building below the hoverbarge. They all take awkward steps, their bodies and limbs bent into odd angles. Two are supported by their comrades. The group huddles together, those with the worst injuries in the middle, and the hoverbarge descends right on top of them. They disappear from view. The craft rises a moment later and the androids are gone.

The two-gunned android in a black trench coat never emerged. The Operator has a feeling he's uninjured, and still marching forward in a relentless, slow-paced pursuit, with the sole purpose of elimination fueling his steps.

Not eager to stick around and find out, the Operator turns and runs through the market, weaving through the crowd until he gets to the smoking lounge. "Take me to them," he says, breathless, to the young male White Jacket still sitting in the back.

The former hostage stands up with a groan. "Third time today," he mutters.

"Wait," the Operator says, ignoring his protests. He goes to the entrance and looks back towards the other side of the market, in the direction he came, making sure the two-gunned android isn't on his tail. Satisfied, he goes back through the lounge and follows the young gang member back to Klepsydra's theater.

"How long does it take to kill a midliner?" Klepsydra says when she sees the Operator. On the stage with her, seated at the table, are Miguel and Gabi. None of the other White Jackets that were with her before are still around.

"I went to the pool hall after," the Operator says. He climbs onto the stage and looks at Miguel. "You two run when they came?"

"Out the back door when we heard them outside the hover-craft," Miguel says. "I don't think they ever saw us."

The Operator stands behind Gabi's chair and hangs the rifle from the headrest before putting his hand on it. "How did you get here?"

"Came through the lounge, same way most people get in touch with the White Jackets," Miguel responds.

"You knew I could find them here?"

"Of course, everyone does. She told me you were here earlier, and that she sent you to kill a midliner." Miguel searches his friend's face and finds nothing telling.

"One killed her nephew." The Operator turns towards Klepsydra. "It's taken care of," he says.

"Did you bring any proof?"

"Proof? Did you want his head? They know not to kill the messenger rats—you'll get your proof when you see them all alive. And clean up the station in a few days so your rats don't go down there."

Klepsydra curses under her breath. She snaps at the young

White Jacket, telling him he'd better go back to the smoking lounge until he's sent to the midline himself.

The young man scurries away.

"So." Klepsydra says, her attention back on the Operator. "Who's after you? These two said they never saw a face."

They both know, having seen the men in the badlands when they came to the Sect, but didn't divulge the information. "There's a man with glasses. Short hair combed to the side. Wears a black trench coat. Don't know his name."

"He have a big fella with him, long hair, guns for hands?" Klepsydra asks.

The Operator nods.

Klepsydra leans back in her chair and laughs. "Oh, you two really stepped in it this time!"

"You *two*? I was in my pool hall, minding my business. It's all him!" Miguel says, pointing at the Operator.

"Well, you're dragged into it now too."

"Who are they?" the Operator says, his patience wearing thin.

"Dr. Julian Howl. He's the upper levels resident scientist, specializing in *enhancements*. Sounds like you've already met his pet project."

"The android with guns for hands," the Operator says under his breath.

"Butler. He's nasty, from what I've heard. Those guns he's got attached to his arms? They're micronized cannons—another Dr. Howl special."

"Okay, so they're after us. You can help protect us, right? Give us somewhere to hide?"

An agitated Klepsydra stands up. "From them! There's nothing we can do."

"I took care of your midliner problem!" the Operator says, slamming his hand on the table.

"It's better for them that you did. If it was up to me I'd get rid of every miserable one of them."

"And you said you'd help if I did!"

"Look," Klepsydra says, putting both hands on the table and looking the Operator in the eye. "It's not that I won't. I *can't.* They're unstoppable."

The Operator stands up and paces. "So there's nothing we can do?"

"I didn't say that. There's somewhere you can go—I just don't know exactly where it is."

"What kind of help is that?"

"Look, there's an android refugee camp. They only exist because they're off the grid altogether. Find them and they can help, or at least point you in the right direction."

"And how are we supposed to find them?"

"There's an android who calls himself the procurement officer. Find him and he'll be able to help."

"Where can I find him?"

"Last I heard he was over in Sigma."

"Sigma," the Operator says with a groan, thinking about the men he's angered in that part of the city. "And we don't have a vehicle anymore. It's going to be a long walk."

Klepsydra sucks air against clenched teeth. "That might be a problem," she says, looking at Miguel.

Miguel lifts his left pant leg and shows a swollen, purple ankle. "I twisted it running away."

An androgynous White Jacket bursts into the theater and runs up to Klepsydra. "We have a problem," they say, catching their breath.

"What is it?" Klepsydra asks.

The White Jacket looks at the Operator, Miguel, and Gabi. Klepsydra says to ignore them.

"Big guy, guns for hands, looking for them in the market."

CHAPTER FOURTEEN

Klepsydra looks like she's seen a ghost. "You have to go," she says, pulling Miguel to his feet.

Miguel tries putting weight on his injured ankle and almost falls. He limps forward, putting as little pressure on his left foot as possible, until he falls into the Operator, placing one arm around his shoulder.

The Operator stares at Klepsydra.

"What? There's no way I'm asking my people to face Butler for you," she says.

"Where are we supposed to go? He can't travel."

"There's a healer halfway between here and Sigma—it's on your way. The stairs in this building lead into the midline. There's a door in the tunnel. Exit there, then climb to the second floor. You'll know it when you find it."

Klepsydra jumps down from the stage and starts jogging towards the exit before she turns around like she forgot something.

"I'll tell them we didn't help you, that should buy you some time. If he'll even bother talking to me. After this, we're even for the midliner."

Klepsydra leaves with the messenger, leaving the Operator, Miguel, and Gabi alone on the stage. The group shuffles forward as fast as Miguel can walk, returning to the staircase. They walk down the concrete steps, turning halfway between each level, and again at each level marker. They pass the level of the walkway, then the ground floor, before descending down two levels' worth of stairs, ending up at a cream-colored metal door secured shut with a thick metal bar resting on two hooks.

Gabi stands next to Miguel and accepts his weight when the Operator steps forward and lifts the metal bar away. He leans it against the wall and pulls the door open. A rush of cold air blows against their faces from the darkness beyond the door.

The Operator takes Miguel's weight and steps through the threshold. Gabi doesn't move.

"Come on, it's just the midline. Nothing to be scared of," the Operator says to her. He's distracted with looking into the darkness.

Gabi doesn't bother pushing away the hair that's flown into her face from the air currents. "It's all my fault," she whispers, choked up.

"All your fault? No, no, it's not."

"Yes, it is!" she yells. The sound disappears into the midline and returns as an echo moments later. "None of this would've happened if I stayed in the orphanage!"

"Gabi," Miguel says, removing himself from the Operator's assistance. He limps forward and places both hands on the girl's shoulders, relying on her support while providing his own to her. "You did nothing wrong. These men are bad; remember that. Bad men do bad things."

She looks past Miguel, at the Operator. "I wish you'd never taken me away from the orphanage," she mutters. "I don't care what my mom did for you!" she says to the Operator through eyes filled with tears.

"We don't have time for this," the Operator says. "Let's go."

"Your mother wanted you safe," says Miguel.

"I was safe before!"

"They were watching you before, waiting to find out why you were kept hostage," the Operator says. "It was only a matter of time until they found out about your secret."

Miguel stands tall, turns around, and puts one hand onto the doorframe for support. "What secret?"

"She can sense androids," the Operator says. "She told Druid she knew about me from the beginning."

Miguel looks at Gabi with a mixture of shock and curiosity. "How? He's the best one I've ever seen. It took me living with him a long time before I realized."

"His whole body glows." She looks down at the ground. "Humans don't."

"And Dr. Howl would've kept you locked away when he discovered what you can do. He's after you now because Druid told him."

"I should've kept my mouth shut," she mutters, crossing her arms.

"Too late for that," the Operator says, reaching his hand out. Gabi takes it and allows him to pull her into the midline. Then, the Operator supports Miguel and helps him through as well before closing the door behind them, submerging them in total darkness.

They start walking towards Sigma, the Operator supporting Miguel and Miguel holding Gabi's hand. "Why would Druid tell them?" Miguel whispers. Sounds seem louder without the use of sight.

"All he cares about is the Sect. Trying to protect it, I guess."

"And putting all of us at risk doesn't matter?"

"That's why you can't trust people," the Operator says.

"We're trusting you," Gabi says.

"I'm repaying a debt."

The group makes slow progress. Pillars and rail lines are distinguishable in the shadows once their eyes become accustomed to the darkness. Miguel stops at regular intervals, leaning against a nearby pillar, or the wall if he can't make it farther.

"What exactly are we looking for?" Gabi asks during one of their breaks. She lifts her leg and puts the sole of her shoe on the pillar, then bounces between leaning forward and standing straight.

"I'm not sure. Klepsydra said there was a door, that's all I know."

"I haven't seen any doors," Gabi says.

"Can either of you even see the walls?" Miguel asks.

All three agree they can't.

"Let's hope it's obvious," Miguel says. "Worst case scenario, we end up in Sigma."

Gabi can't ignore the futility of their search when they continue walking. "What if we walk right by it?"

"We won't."

"What if they can't do anything for him?"

"They will."

"What if they can, and they won't because they're scared of Butler too?"

"We won't tell them that part."

"Unless he shows up . . ." Gabi says.

"He won't show up."

"How do you know though?"

The Operator lets her question hang in the air. Miguel slips on a loose rock, stumbling forward and putting pressure on his left foot. He groans in pain.

"This isn't getting any easier," Miguel says.

"We've got to be close," the Operator says.

"How do you *know*?" Gabi shoots back.

The Operator calms himself with a deep breath. Then, he walks Miguel to the closest pillar. "Stay here," he says. "I'm going ahead to find this place."

He walks away and hears Gabi's quick footsteps behind him. "Stay with Miguel," the Operator says. Her outline is frozen for a brief instant before she turns around and stomps back.

The Operator breaks into a steady jog, thinking he can run all the way to Sigma if he needs to—then, he'll know if the door's obvious or finding it requires more careful inspection. His breathing becomes heavier while his eyes scan both sides, careful he doesn't stumble on the tracks. A strange smell, one he doesn't recognize right away, invades his nostrils. He knows he's smelled it before but can't place it. It disappears when he continues running, but the persistence of the distant memory overtakes his search for the door and he turns around.

Finding where the scent is strongest, he feels the ground for its origin. Nothing but the rails. He moves towards a wall, finding that the scent weakens on that side. The scent is stronger towards the opposite wall.

An added sweetness to the smell transports him back in time, to when he was younger and worked in the upper levels. His office was next to the horticulture splicers—he realizes this particular sweetness is from flowers. In an instant he places the other: fresh earth and greenery. His nose leads him to a door. Pushing it in, he discovers a world of green inside a staircase illuminated by artificial light, the heavy scent of living plants carried on bright, fresh air.

He pulls the door shut harder than he meant to, and the sound echoes off the walls around him.

Miguel and Gabi are where he left them. He helps Miguel to his feet and tells Gabi it's time they continued.

"Did you find it?" Gabi says.

"I think so."

The Operator follows the scent to the door again and opens it wide. The light from inside hurts their eyes, and Gabi peers through her fingers at the lush greenery.

"Who can afford all this?" she asks.

"It's not expensive if you grow it yourself," Miguel answers.

"People grow this stuff?" she says. She pulls a vine close to her face and sniffs. Then, she moves to a closed flower, leans forward, and breathes in through her nose. "That smells really good," she says, a sheepish smile pasted on her lips.

"Let's go," the Operator says, helping Miguel climb the stairs.

"So these plants belong to the healer?" Gabi says.

"I think so," the Operator responds.

"How can plants heal people?" she mutters, more to herself than anyone else.

"Because, they have magical properties!" a booming voice says from above.

The Operator withdraws his blaster and aims it at the next landing.

"No need for the weapons, boy, you came to me!"

"Can you help an injured old man?" Miguel yells out to the air above.

"Come up and find out!"

The Operator looks at Miguel. They both shrug, then he puts his blaster away.

On the second floor, they find a short woman with red curly hair and large eyes magnified through glasses. Next to her, attached to the railing, is a megaphone sitting on an attached box.

"The voice usually scares away the ones who don't really need my help," she explains. Her actual voice is high-pitched—she sounds younger than Gabi. She looks at Miguel's foot without being told the problem.

"You've done a number on yourself, friend."

"I know," Miguel says. His face softens when she addresses him, and he smiles in a way the Operator hasn't seen before.

Gabi looks at him and rolls her eyes.

"Let's take a look."

The healer leads them through a large room with rows and rows of all-sized plants to a small room with a padded table.

"Lay on here," she says.

Miguel does, and she lifts his pant leg. He winces when she presses his purple ankle.

"I'll have to make a splint," she says.

"Out of the plants?" Gabi asks.

"No," the Healer says with a laugh. "Those are mostly for decoration. It's an advanced plastic that forms to the ankle, reinforces the soft tissues, and dulls the pain. Like a mini-exoskeleton." The Healer holds up a piece of shimmering green material. "He'll be good as new. I'll make it as soon as I get back," she says while standing up and slinging a bag over her shoulder.

The Operator positions himself in front of her. "Get back? We need him fixed as soon as possible."

"Why? Got a hot date?" the Healer says. She turns to Miguel and winks.

"No, there's—" Gabi begins.

"Yes, we do," the Operator says, cutting her off. "In Sigma."

"It's going to take a few hours, I can do it after I deliver this medicine," she says, pushing the Operator aside.

The Operator reaches his hand out. "Let me take it for you."

Suspicious eyes search the Operator's face before she shrugs. "Okay," the Healer says, holding out her bag. "But I'll break his other leg if I find out anything happens."

Miguel laughs until the Healer turns around; her locked jaw wipes his smile away.

CHAPTER FIFTEEN

THE THIRD PORTION of the city, Theta district, takes up the entirety of the city's real estate next to the bay. It's a long, thin strip of land with cleaner air because of the breeze coming from the water. Access to the area isn't straightforward—like the other two districts, they prefer isolation. The few people who travel between the districts risk trips through the tunnels, despite widespread fear of the midliners. Under normal circumstances, the Operator would travel to Theta using the same method. However, the Healer, in her old age, doesn't make the trip belowground, and she tells him about a special access point created for her by Theta's powerful citizens that need the medicine.

The Operator approaches a wall of cars and junk metal. Decades of stagnation have melded the entire structure into one. He stands in front of the specified wall, waiting for the gatekeeper. The buildings in and around Theta don't have the same hyper-commercialized exteriors. Instead of bright neon lights flashing advertisements about various products and companies at the citizens, they hang banners down from a variety of heights. The ones closest to the surface are readable through the haze, but reading the banners higher up is difficult without the colored accents of those in Gamma. The middle of every banner ripples as it catches a breeze—both ends are secured against the building.

WestCorp has the highest concentration of hanging banners, identifiable by their green block letters on a light grey background. They make everything from baby bottles to gaming systems for those on the higher levels, the people who don't even know the different districts exist and don't bother with the territorial struggles of those below the reclaimers.

A child's head appears above the wall of scrap metal while the Operator reads the banners in the distance. "Hello," the boy calls down.

"Medicine delivery," the Operator says, tapping the satchel on his side.

"You're not Agota," the child says, disappointed. "Where is she?"

"She sent me."

An older version of the boy, no more than a teenager, appears. They could be clones if it wasn't for the missing nostrils.

It's the first time the Operator's seen Theta's typical body modification, and he's both intrigued and repulsed.

"How are we supposed to know that?" the teenager says.

"This is her bag, isn't it?" the Operator says, turning to his side and showing it to them.

The two boys inspect him from above for a brief moment before the younger version turns around and yells, "Dad!"

A third version of the same face, missing nostrils like the teenager but with a salt-and-pepper beard, appears over the barrier.

"He says Agota sent him," the teenager says, never taking his eyes off the Operator.

"She did," the Operator says. A moment of silence passes. "Do you want to be the reason the medicine doesn't get delivered?"

The oldest version shakes his head no. "Open it up," he says, his voice tinged with a hint of defeat.

A thin door indistinguishable from the scrapped cars opens in the center of the scrap-metal barrier. The young boy holds the door open while the Operator passes through, walks through the barrier, then through another open door made of gleaming metal on the far side.

"Thanks," the Operator says to the teenager holding the second door.

The father stands in the barrier's shadow with his arms crossed, staring at the Operator. All three Theta occupants wear the same outfit—billowing tan pants, a cream-colored shirt, and a dark brown belt. "I'll escort you."

"That won't be necessary. Agota told me where to go," the Operator says. He hadn't known the healer's name before the child revealed it.

"I wasn't asking," the father said. His hand goes down to the gun on his hip.

The Operator chuckles, unfazed by the threat. "Suit yourself."

"Stay here, boys," the father says to his kids.

Both Sigma and Gamma districts don't bother refacing their barriers, leaving the decrepit metal for decades and adding to it whenever the structure needs support. Theta district, however, has covered theirs with sheets of shiny metal. The aesthetic carries over to the rest of their territory as well. Instead of abandoned and vandalized storefronts interspersed with barricaded windows, they have installed thick glass panes on all windows and keep unused areas empty. There's no graffiti and no trash on the ground. The buildings' shadows still create a cool darkness below the reclaimers, but the reduced haze because of the water's breeze means looking into the distance isn't a fruitless endeavor. The men they pass as they walk farther into Theta district all wear the same outfit as the barrier's guardians, and the women wear cream-colored dresses with a brown belt. Everyone's brown boots look sturdy enough for a trip through the midline.

They turn left and walk towards a series of crowded establishments. Lounging residents, all of their nostrils cut, sit at tables set up on the sidewalk and in the street. Some are eating, some reading, and others engaged in intense conversation. As they're walking through, the Operator sees a young man with a computer in front of him take a vial from his pocket and jam it into his arm before diving back into his work with renewed focus.

The escort follows the Operator's gaze. "Don't use much Stim on the ground where you're from?" he says. "We don't like letting the upper levels have all the fun."

Bacas made sure Gamma's residents didn't have the chance for the increased productivity generated by Stim addiction, keeping the supply from the government for himself and his gang. Everyone in Gamma got used to drinking Serum, a Stim derivative. The Operator, who swore off Stim once he broke the habit, can't decide who has the right attitude towards the substance.

They turn down an empty street, walking towards the bay in the distance. There's something about the expanse beyond, the lack of landmarks, that makes the Operator uneasy. It reminds the Operator of the badlands but feels different. As an android, has he been programmed with an aversion to water?

There are a number of heavy steel doors on each side of the street, with thick windows on the second and third floors. He gets the sense he's being watched and remembers walking into the White Jackets' side of town in search of a poker game on his first day back in the city. The escort stops outside a door on the right, indistinguishable from the rest, and knocks three times.

A barrel-chested man with a bushy beard opens the door. "What do you want?" he says. He takes a big breath through his nose, drawing attention to his lack of nostrils. His dark purple outfit is the same style as the escort's, just a different color.

The escort pushes the Operator forward.

"Medicine delivery," the Operator says.

The doorman looks at the bag then nods. The Operator steps inside before the door closes in the escort's face.

The building's interior reminds the Operator he's still in the same city. The carpet in the entrance is shabby and worn, with holes missing from years of foot traffic. So many crystals are missing from the chandelier above that halving the size would still leave missing interstices. The stairs he walks up creak and groan from the combined weight of him and the door-man, and on the ascent to the second level, the doorman tells the Operator not to step on a particular stair because it's "having issues."

They walk down a hall and end up at a large wooden door. The doorman walks in without knocking and the Operator follows. Inside, a young mother watches a child no more than four play with colored blocks. Neither have nostrils. A loose piece of purple cloth hangs over purple sheets on a massive canopy bed on the far side of the room.

"Leave it on the table," the doorman says.

The Operator sets his satchel down on the small circular table near the door and begins pulling out the small flasks. There are a dozen total. In the background, he hears both mother and child wheezing.

"Thank you," the mother says. Her voice is scratchy.

The child sneezes, then closes his eyes with a grimace. "I

know it hurts, honey. Take this." She approaches the table, takes one of the flasks, and makes the child drink.

Once the liquid passes through the child's throat, he takes a big breath through his nose.

"Let's go," the doorman says, pulling the Operator's arm. The Operator doesn't move. The two men stare at each other before the Operator grabs the empty satchel, puts it over his shoulder, and walks out.

The escort isn't outside. The Operator remembers the path back to the access point, so he sets off on his own. The feeling of being watched pervades his thoughts. Keeping his eyes forward with deliberate intent, he marches on until he turns the corner. Once there, he freezes when he discovers not a single soul still sits outside.

A white piece of trash, a food wrapper left behind from someone's meal, blows across the dining space. A man appears in the distance, on the opposite side of the seating area. He's wearing a khaki jumpsuit, a black face mask, and a black hat. He takes off his hat and shows a shock of blond hair—Ludavico's brother, the security guard.

"Didn't think I would track you down?" the man yells.

The Operator's hand goes down to his gun. "How did you find me over here?" he says.

"We don't just make sure the trash stays below the third level . . . we also make sure you stay where you belong! Can't have people crossing districts and causing trouble."

Security must not know about, or bother with, midline travel.

The breeze comes in off the ocean, swirling around both men. All of a sudden, the guard withdraws his blaster and fires. At the same instant, the Operator pulls out his blaster and shoots the guard in the chest.

The incoming shot flies past the Operator's head.

Lucavico's brother stumbles backwards, then begins firing shots in rapid succession while surging forward.

The Operator dives out of the way, his satchel trailing behind him, and scrambles to refuge behind the corner of a building.

"How much Stim did you take?" the Operator calls out.

"Enough to get the job done!" Ludavico's brother answers. Shots pour into the building's corner, creating a cloud of stone dust.

The Operator waves his hand in front of his face, dispersing the particles in the air. "No wonder you missed me at the crossing. You're a terrible shot!" he yells.

The guard roars.

The Operator counts to three, spacing out the numbers according to an internal clock he doesn't question. When he hits one, he throws himself to the ground onto his left side, his head just past the corner. He brings his right arm up and fires three shots into the guard's chest, who now stands two tables away. The fourth shot lands between the man's eyes and he falls backwards as if in slow motion.

After standing up and dusting himself off, the Operator checks the satchel. There's a finger-sized hole through the side.

Shaking his head, the Operator approaches his attacker and stands over the man. He bends down and takes the guard's blaster pistol, putting it into the satchel and carrying it with him back through the barrier separating Theta and Gamma.

CHAPTER SIXTEEN

"AND AFTER WE put the seeds into the hole we made with our finger, we fill it with dirt. Yes, just like that," the healer says, her calm voice audible from the hall.

The Operator walks into the room that houses the healer's rows of plants. Gabi and the healer are on their knees next to a large pot, their hands in the dirt. Miguel is on the far side, behind the plants, walking tall while testing out his stabilized ankle. Hazy sunlight, the day's last rays, pours in from a wall of windows that were closed before.

"Welcome back," Miguel says with a smile. He lifts his hands higher than the plants and points down in satisfaction.

"Feel all right?" the Operator asks.

"Better than all right!" Miguel answers.

The healer stands up and brushes the dirt from her hands on a cream-colored apron that hangs from her waist, adding to its array of brown stains. "Did you drop off the medicine?"

"I did."

"Any problems?"

The Operator pauses for a moment, recalling the shoot-out. "None whatsoever. What are you guys doing here?" he says, directing his question at Gabi. She pours water on the seeds using a dented bright blue metal watering can.

When Gabi doesn't respond right away, absorbed in her task, the healer replies that they're growing new plants.

Gabi sets the watering can down and pats the moistened soil. She stands up and looks at her dirty hands.

"Here," the healer says, offering her apron. Gabi rubs dirt on both sides.

The Operator takes the satchel off his shoulder and gives it to the healer. "What's in here?" she says. She peers in then squeezes the fabric satchel shut. "What am I supposed to do with this?"

"Since I returned your bag with a hole in it. Do you have one already?" the Operator asks.

The apprehensive healer shakes her head.

"What is it?" Miguel says, walking to the others from across the room.

Gabi's curious gaze focuses on the satchel.

"A blaster," the Operator says. "In case her voice-change doesn't work on unwanted visitors."

"I don't know . . ."

"Just in case. We each have one too," the Operator says, patting the blaster at his side. His heart drops when he realizes he left the blaster rifle at the theater, hanging on the chair.

"Keep it hidden," Miguel offers. "Point and shoot when you need it. Most of the time, just pointing it is enough to get the message across."

"I'll think about it." A moment later, she thanks the Operator. "Where did you get it?"

"Found it on the ground. It still works."

The healer looks at him like she doesn't believe him, but turns around and walks back into the room where she fixed Miguel.

"The ankle feels good?" The Operator asks his friend.

"Can't even tell I ever injured it! It feels stiff—not the ankle itself, but the brace." Miguel lifts up his pant leg and shows the Operator the shimmering green metal splint. "But I can walk just fine."

"Good, we've got to get going."

The healer returns from the back room and hands Gabi a small packet. "Here are some seeds for you. Just find some dirt and plant them where they can see the sun, just like I showed you."

Gabi accepts the seeds with two hands and puts them into her pocket.

"Keep those hidden, so nobody finds out," the Operator says, as if the seeds are precious cargo.

"Could you do me a favor?" the healer asks Miguel, her voice laced with an added sweetness. He nods, and she continues. "Could you bring back the brace? I can reuse the metal," she says.

Miguel blushes. "Of course. I'd love to come back."

"Other than that, we're even. I hate making the walk to Theta," the healer says to the Operator. She then turns her attention back to her plants. She withdraws a small pair of pruning shears from a back pocket and begins inspecting nearby leaves.

The Operator, Miguel, and Gabi all say goodbye and show themselves out, heading back down to the midline. They shut the door on the illuminated stairwell crowded with plants and stare into the darkness. They aren't walking long before Miguel says that he has something to tell the Operator.

"Don't make a big deal out of it," Miguel says.

"I won't."

"Well, I didn't want to say anything before . . ."

"About what?"

"Because I'm fine without it."

The Operator stops walking. "What is it?"

"I don't have a blaster," Miguel says.

"Wait, what? What about the one we took off the guys who trashed the pool hall?"

"I left it behind when Dr. Howl and everyone came."

"It was on the kitchen counter when we left," Gabi adds. "Just sitting there."

The Operator thinks about the pool hall's back room; he doesn't remember seeing the weapon. "They must have taken it," he says.

"Either way, it's not a big deal. I'll be fine."

"Until you're not. We've got to get you some protection."

"Where do you get one? Is there a store?" Gabi asks.

"There's a stall in the market in Gamma," Miguel says. "I don't know about in Sigma."

The Operator stops. The other two do too when they realize he's no longer walking.

"We can't go back there," Miguel says. "Let's just keep going to Sigma."

"Nobody will sell us one. They'll know we aren't from Sigma right away."

"Why do you say that?" Gabi asks.

"They all have pointed teeth. The second we talk they'll know."

"I told you, I don't need one," Miguel reiterates.

"Where would you go in Gamma if you wanted a blaster without anyone finding out? Is there a black market?" the Operator asks when they've resumed walking.

Miguel doesn't talk for a moment. The only sound is their footsteps, two pairs of grown-man strides and the quickened patter of Gabi's. "Couldn't have gone to the casino—the Enforcers were in charge of that. Maybe one of the clubs?"

"There's a club in Gamma?" the Operator asks.

"Oh yeah. It's where all the young White Jackets used to gather. Never knew quite where it was—they kept a lid on it so Bacas wouldn't shut it down."

"And you think you could buy a gun there?"

"That's how they first sold Serum—traded it for weapons. This was before Bacas realized he could use their creation for his own advantage."

They get to Sigma district as the sun retreats behind the skyscrapers. The streetlights tick on one at a time, with many staying dark. The flashing neon lights from above play upon the surface, dancing in the haze.

"Keep your mouth shut," the Operator tells Gabi and Miguel.

"I didn't say anything," Gabi hisses.

"No, so nobody sees your normal teeth. And Miguel, keep those big blue eyes on the ground."

"I'll be careful," he grumbles.

The Operator leads his group back to the intersection where he found the street races, aware of how those who run it feel about him—they made it clear when they fired the rocket at his hovercraft. He plans to stay at the fringes and gather information, and doesn't know anywhere else he could find news about Sigma's club. But, when they arrive, there's nobody there except a gray-haired old man wearing a sports jacket and a black knee-length skirt walking with his orange cat on a leash. Any rats the pair encounters run away when the cat prances close to them.

"Excuse me," Miguel says to the old man before the Operator can stop him. "Where do all the young kids spend their time and money late into the night?"

The old man and his cat look at Miguel at the same time. "If they're not at a damned race, they're wasting their nights at Chance."

"Chance?"

"It's a bar. Dark, loud—perfect when you're young, intolerable once you've got some sense." He inspects Miguel and his group. "You three will never get in," he says. Both he and his cat turn away with a dramatic flourish, continuing on their way.

"Where is it?" Miguel calls after him.

The man points in the direction he's walking. The Operator, Miguel, and Gabi follow him for a while, before they watch him go into a ruined building, one of the few they've encountered that doesn't extend above the third-level reclaimers.

People crowd around the entrance to Chance, some in line and others lying on the sidewalk outside, inebriated. Vibrations from heavy bass fill the block.

"Sounds like a dance club to me," Miguel says as the trio get in line.

The scene reminds the Operator of Suerte, Bacas's former casino in Gamma.

"She can't come in," the bouncer says when the Operator and his group are at the front of the line. A permanent scowl on a thin-lipped mouth sits higher than the Operator's head, and the bouncer's shirt seams are tight against his broad shoulders. He looks into Chance before returning his attention to the trio. "Make a decision," he says to them, "I don't have all night."

Miguel says he'll stay with Gabi outside and shuffles her away before the Operator can utter any disagreements. The bouncer shoves him inside.

Inside the bar, it's as if someone condensed the outside atmosphere and charged it with electricity. The air is so thick it's like walking through a cloud, complete with a measure of moisture that saturates the Operator's tongue. In the city streets, the billboards high above the surface cast down flashing neon lights; inside Chance, those billboard colors are on the ceiling and every wall. The people inside pulsate in time with the rhythm of the music and lights, creating a writhing mass of sticky bodies.

The Operator finds the bar and squeezes his way to the counter, hurrying so the unarmed Miguel and Gabi spend as little time as possible without his protection. One of the bartenders, a young woman with the bare minimum amount of fabric covering her body, hands him a drink.

"Here ya go, hon," she says, leaning forward with her hands on the bar and squeezing her arms together. Her pointed teeth glow in the dim light.

"I don't get to order?" the Operator says.

"Nobody gets anything but Gamma Serum since the Enforcer stopped keeping it for himself," she says, dismissing the question. "Want me to open a tab for ya?"

The Operator nods and takes out a red plastic disk—the standard color for up to five million credits. "What would you say if you met the guy who put Gamma Serum back on the menu?"

The bartender stands tall and rubs her hands down her hips, pressing against her thighs as she pulls them back up. "I'd thank him for keeping me paid."

The Operator nods while he rolls the disk over his fingers. "And what if I was looking for a blaster?"

The bartender looks him in the eye and walks away, her head twisting as she does so she can maintain her suggestive gaze until the last possible second. The Operator turns around with his drink in his hand and leans his back against the bar. He nods his head along with the beat, wondering if the street race organizers ever come to the establishment.

All of a sudden, a thick arm closes around his neck and drags him to the other side of the bar.

"That's the one!" the flirtatious bartender yells.

"You've got to go," a gruff voice says right behind the Operator's ear. "No Enforcers allowed in here."

The Operator reaches down and pulls the man's blaster from its holster. He shoots the man in the foot, then stands up, wheezing and massaging his throat. The sound of the shot is lost in the music.

"I'm not an Enforcer," he croaks.

"You were looking for a blaster so you can pin us for gun running!" the bartender shouts. An inebriated patron shouts at her, saying he wants two more drinks. "Go to hell," she says, spitting at him. The spit hits the man in the face and he rubs it in, delighting in the sensation.

CHAPTER SEVENTEEN

THE OPERATOR KEEPS the bouncer's gun trained on him at hip height—hidden from the patrons at the bar—while the man stands up, his weight supported by both hands on the bar's counter. The bartender rushes forward and pulls one of his arms off the counter before putting it around her shoulder, supporting him. She helps him to the back with the Operator following, still aiming at the pair.

"You're going to pay for this," the bouncer snarls as the door swings closed behind the Operator. The unoccupied room they enter has four padded red chairs around a coffee table sitting beneath a crystal chandelier. There are more padded chairs along the room's red walls, and the soft yellow lights reflecting off the large mirror gives the room a tranquil glow.

More bouncers stream in from a side door. They all unholster their weapons when they see the Operator holding their colleagues at gunpoint.

"Shoot him!" the injured bouncer says.

"Don't," says the calm voice of a man who enters the room last. He's wearing an all-black suit, with a black shirt and tie.

"He's an Enforcer!" the bartender yells.

"No, I'm not. I'm just looking for a blaster," the Operator replies.

"Looks like you've already got two," the man in black says with a nod to the Operator's holster.

"I'm looking to buy another." The Operator lets the barrel drop and the blaster spins backwards, the trigger guard resting on the Operator's finger.

"Why wouldn't I just tell my men to shoot you now?"

"You could. But then you'll be killing the man who made selling Gamma Serum possible."

The bartender chuckles, her chest straining against the minuscule pieces of fabric. "This again," she says. She looks at the man in black. "He was talking about the man who put Serum back on the menu."

"I did. I'm the one who killed the Enforcer who was hoarding the stuff. And also the one who opened up Gamma— do you think Bacas would've let you get the Serum so easily if he was still around?"

The man in black crosses his arms. "Elaborate."

"Is that a memory mirror?" the Operator says, reaching into his pocket and pulling out the thimble he took from the antique cash register in the furniture stall back in Gamma. He shakes it in his hand like it's a pair of dice.

"It is," the man in black responds.

"Can I?"

"Please do."

The Operator slips the thimble onto his left index finger and places it on his temple. All of a sudden, the mirror lights up and displays the world through the Operator's eyes. Everyone in the room watches, in double speed, how the Operator walked into Sigma from the midline, went up to the Enforcer's room on the tenth level, and shot the man through the heart. The Operator skips forward in time, to when Bacas stood over him, and shows Gamma's chief Enforcer being shot in the face.

Nobody says a word when the Operator pulls the thimble from his temple and puts it back in his pocket. They all stare at him, unsure.

"Get out," the man in black says to his cronies. He points at the injured bouncer. "Someone help him," he says, before telling the bartender to get back behind the bar. Alone with the Operator, he introduces himself. "My name is Regulo Pavlova; this is my bar."

"I'm looking to buy a blaster," the Operator says, getting straight to the point.

Pavlova holds out his hand and accepts the injured bouncer's blaster from him. "Unfortunately, I can't part with this one —it's his personal weapon. And Sigma's Enforcers crack down on illegal weapon sales; they're always in here fishing, trying to catch us breaking the law."

The Operator stays silent, waiting for the conclusion of the man's rambling.

"But, I do have a broken one you're welcome to have. It's the old style, uses real bullets—not the energy shot these new weapons shoot. Come with me," he says, turning around and waving his hand.

He leads the Operator to an office farther away from the club's main floor. The bass from the music vibrates throughout the room at a fraction of its true intensity. Pavlova sets the bouncer's weapon next to the computer on his desk before opening a desk drawer and pulling out an ancient revolver, silver with a bone-white handle. "I don't have any ammo for it," he says as he hands over the weapon. "There's an abandoned underground mall nearby that's been converted into a dump. The trash pickers might be able to point you in the right direction for some."

The Operator takes the weapon and aims it at the wall. "You don't have anything energy-based I could buy? Or know where I could get one?"

"No. Finding guns for my men takes days, sometimes weeks. This is all I have right now."

"How much do you want for it?" the Operator says, pulling the weapon down and holding it at his side.

"It's yours, for opening up the pipeline to Gamma Serum."

"Thanks. We appreciate it."

"We?"

The Operator tells him about Miguel and Gabi, still outside the club. "Is there somewhere they could stay while I look for ammo for this?" he asks.

"I can't have a child in the club, but there are rooms in the next building—they're mine too. I'll give you a good rate on my personal room."

The Operator hands over the red disk filled with credits and Pavlova hands him a plastic key card with a large letter P on the top.

"This will get you into the building too," Pavlova says before giving him directions to the trash pickers' domain. "Let me know if you ever need anything else."

"There is one thing," the Operator says. "Do you know where I can get in touch with a guy who calls himself the procurement officer?"

Pavlova laughs. "Yes, I know him. We work together often, and he owes me more than a few favors. I'll have him swing by the room."

The Operator considers asking Pavlova about the android refugee camp but decides against it, trusting Klepsydra's directions. She knew what she was talking about with the healer, after all.

"Last thing: Do you have anything to do with the street races?"

"No. Those are run by the Dominguez brothers. We stay out of each other's way."

"Got it. Thanks again," the Operator says before walking out, leaving the club owner alone in his office.

Miguel and Gabi are laughing together when the Operator walks up to them.

"What's so funny?"

They both stand up. "We're just imagining other body mods besides pointed teeth and blue eyes," Miguel says with a wink to his friend. "Did you get another blaster?"

"An old-school one. I've got to find ammo for it. In the meantime, you two can stay in the Chance owner's room."

Miguel whistles, impressed.

The building next to Chance is a run-down former upscale hotel, with frayed ornate chairs and broken mirrors on the walls. A concierge android without synthetic skin surrounding its metal skeleton asks for their key, and once it's received says he'll take them to their room.

"I'll be back," the Operator tells Miguel and Gabi, leaving them with the concierge android and turning back out of the building.

The entrance to the underground mall is a curved archway set in a skyscraper. The outside edge is rusted metal, and pieces of broken glass still stick to the arch's highest points. A continuous pile of scrap metal lines both sides of a narrow walkway, illuminated by firelight in the distance. Rats scurry among the piles, getting out of the Operator's way when he enters the converted space.

A metal railing marks the end of the corridor—beyond is a vast open space. The walkway splits in two, running along the inside edge of the railing with the scrap metal forming the outer barrier. The Operator pauses at the railing, looking into the abandoned mall. He's two levels up. The visible space in the middle of the bottom level has a small fire burning, reminding him of one of his campsites in the badlands. The middle level has trash piled waist high, organized into different types. The abandoned mall's uppermost level has heaps of scrap metal piled to the ceiling.

The Operator spots the staircase and travels to it while searching for potential threats. He's about to descend the staircase when a person clearing their throat behind him makes him turn around.

"You're not going to say hello?"

The Operator looks around for whoever spoke.

"Up here."

It's a young man, lounging on the top of the scrap metal with one leg crossed over the other. He's wiry, with messed-up hair and skin covered in grease. In one graceful leap, he's on the walkway with the Operator.

The Operator kicks himself for assuming there wasn't enough room above the scrap metal for a human.

"What brings you in here?" the trash picker asks, twirling a pencil-sized piece of metal between his fingers.

"Looking for ammo," the Operator says, pulling out the revolver.

"Whew, that's nice. I've got a ton." The young man nods his head towards the staircase and leads the Operator down.

"How much does it cost?" the Operator says, thinking about his limited credits after paying for the room.

"Cost? You're doing us a favor takin' it off our hands! We can't exactly melt it down or else it'll explode. And nobody uses the old-style guns anymore." He stops walking, leans close to the Operator, and holds his hand up to his mouth. When the Operator doesn't move, he beckons with his hand and widens his eyes. The Operator acquiesces.

"They said I was crazy for saving it. But I figured someone could use it someday!" he whispers.

"You are crazy!" a voice yells from behind a pile of nearby trash.

"Quit your hollerin' and mind yer own business!" the young man yells towards the source of the noise. Turning back to the Operator, he says, "Come on."

As they walk across the open space in the middle of the bottom floor, the Operator looks up at the distant railing where he first took it all in. The small cooking fire is untended, and there isn't anyone around. "Where is everyone?" he asks.

"In their hideouts. We only come here for meals and whatnot."

The trash picker leads the Operator to six metal barrels sawed in half just within the light from the fire. Inside each are piles of ammo of all different shapes and sizes.

"Take as much as you want!" the proud young man says, slapping the Operator on the back.

The Operator takes out the pistol. "Do you have anything that fits this gun?" he asks.

"I sure do!" He points into the barrels. "Somewhere in there."

Kneeling down, the Operator tries a bullet that looks like it could match. It slides in but his gun doesn't close.

"I'm going to grab some grub. You want any?" the young trash picker asks.

"No, thanks."

"Suit yourself!"

The Operator grabs another bullet out of the thousands present before checking if it fits in the revolver, settling in for a long night.

CHAPTER EIGHTEEN

HOURS INTO HIS SEARCH, the Operator has discovered a handful of bullets that fit into the revolver. Most are tarnished, some with rust spots, though there are a few gleaming specimens in the pile. He shuffles through the top layer for ammo that works instead of working through entire half barrels of random bullets, since there is no extra container for the ammo he's already searched through—a lesson learned when he had to clean up unsuitable bullets from the floor after searching through the first barrel.

A handful of trash pickers emerged during his search, every one of them thin and covered in grease. They all approached the small fire, taking turns keeping it alive while they cooked their meals. A young mother with a small child and baby in her arms stayed for a while because her son was interested in the Operator's daunting task. The son sat in his squat and tried bullets that were the same size as what the Operator specified. Despite coming up with a substantial mound of options, just two worked.

The Operator stands up and stretches, his hands on his hips while he leans back. He looks across the mall's expanse at the large store on the far side's middle level. Takahari, the electronics brand, their aged sign forever turned off and illuminated by a dim emergency light nobody bothered turning off. He settles back down onto his knees and attacks the last two half barrels.

A trove of suitable bullets emerges midway through the last half barrel. Handfuls of the ammo, shining like new, are withdrawn from the rich seam. Exposing them requires transferring the upper layers of bullets to the other five half barrels until they're overflowing; some spill onto the floor. The Operator slips a handful into his pocket when he's uncovered all he can then stands up, cracking his back by twisting left and right. Exhausted, he lies down next to the pile of suitable ammo on the floor and closes his eyes for a quick nap.

"You find what you were looking for?" the young trash picker says hours later.

The Operator, his eyes still closed, hears him as if he's far away.

The trash picker repeats himself, louder. "Did you find—"

"Yes, yes I did," the Operator says without opening his eyes.

"Good. I knew there was a reason I kept those!" A moment later, the young man asks if the Operator wants any breakfast.

The Operator opens his eyes and sees the young man's back, blocking the fire from view. "What are you making?"

"Just cooking up some rats," he replies.

The midliner's chosen meal. "Sure, I'll take one," the Operator says. The concept of eating rodents stopped bothering him after he ate nothing else while recovering with Usryd from Bacas's torture.

"One? I'm not gonna make you work through all those small bones. This here's a stew."

The Operator sits up. "Is it morning?" he asks, surprised at how tired he feels.

"Close enough. Sun's about to come up."

"How do you know?"

"Because I woke up," the young man says, as if the answer's obvious.

The Operator sits up and leans against one of the ammo barrels. Before long, he's handed a bowl of a thin stew with little besides small pieces of meat. "Thanks," he says.

"Tell me what you think," the young man says, staring at the Operator, waiting for his guest's first bite.

The Operator takes a wary spoonful of the stuff and lets it sit in his mouth. He's grateful the taste is almost nonexistent. "It's good," he says.

The young trash picker beams with pride.

"I was waiting for people to wake up—I want to see how this thing shoots," the Operator says, holding the revolver up.

"You didn't need to wait for anyone! They make noise all times of the day. Plus, people throw scrap metal in here and make a racket no matter the time—in the middle of the night if it suits them. Trust me, we're all used to it."

"A gunshot's louder than some metal hitting the floor."

"You'd be surprised," a voice says from somewhere on the middle level.

"Come on, I wanna watch," the young man says. He leads the Operator through the open space in the middle of the mall, closer to the abandoned Takahari store, then points at the sign. "We can see what you hit here," he says.

The Operator takes six bullets from his pocket and loads them into the revolver. Taking aim at the *T*, he fires. The sound of the shot reverberates off the walls in the empty mall, followed by the sound of plastic and glass hitting the floor from the damaged sign.

"Woo!" the trash picker yells. "That was amazing! Do it again."

The Operator replaces the blaster in his holster with the revolver, slipping the blaster into the back of his pants. Then, with his hand hovering over the weapon, he takes a deep breath before withdrawing the gun and firing a shot into the *A*, *K*, *A*, *H*, and *A*.

"Now *that* was awesome," the trash picker says, clapping the Operator on the back. "Can I try?"

The Operator loads another six bullets into the gun. "Have you shot a gun before?"

"Blasters, never this kind," he says.

"There's more kick," the Operator says.

"And it's definitely louder," the trash picker observes. "Nobody's still asleep!"

"I thought you said it didn't matter."

"It doesn't. Who's going to say anything to the man with the gun?" He takes aim at the sign and pulls the trigger. The gun kicks up high and the sound of shattered glass hitting the ground adds to the echos in the open space.

"This thing's come alive!" He lines up another shot. This time, ready for the recoil, the gun stays steady. His shot hits above the second *A*. He shoots through the rest of the rounds and hands over the revolver. "It's fun, but I'd still take a blaster."

"Me too," the Operator says. He slips the revolver into his holster and pulls out his own blaster and fires a shot into every letter of the Takahari sign. "Much smoother."

"Let me feel the difference," the young man says.

The Operator hands over his blaster and watches as the trash picker fires four shots before finding the *T*.

All of a sudden, the young man stops firing. His head creeps forward, his eyes squinting. "There's something moving in the store," he says. Then, a second later, he whispers, "It's a person." He hands the blaster back to the Operator.

The Operator doesn't see a thing and wonders how the trash

picker sees into the store's darkness. As he watches, a heavy boot kicks away the rest of the broken glass and the man it belongs to steps through, exposed in the dim light. The person has long hair spilling onto his shoulders and wears a black trench coat.

Butler.

The Operator pushes the young trash picker with his left hand while falling away to his right, putting more distance between them just as the two-gunned android raises both arms and starts firing.

The shots hit the floor right behind where they stood.

"Run!" the Operator yells. The young man doesn't need telling—he's scrambling on all fours to the shadows under the above level's walkway. The Operator does the same, bullets striking the floor where his feet were moments before. Beneath the walkway, he runs back in the direction of the small fire and ammo he spent all night gathering.

Butler jumps down onto the first level with a thud. The Operator slides behind a pile of scrap metal in the shadows beyond the ammo barrels. The young trash picker emerges on the far side of the fire. He points at the ammo. The Operator nods. Then, all of a sudden, the young man stands up and hits a junked industrial mixer with a short metal rod. The noise draws Butler's attention, and the two-gunned android shoots a continuous barrage of shots while walking forward. The Operator slides his blaster into the back of his pants and takes a series of rapid breaths before running across the open space between his hiding spot and the ammo. He slides feetfirst behind the barrels as the shots start raining down on his protection.

As the Operator loads the collected ammo into his pockets, Butler's shots work through the barrels' exterior and strike the loose bullets. The odds of any loose bullets being struck at the perfect angle, setting them off, is minuscule, but the Operator doesn't want to be there to find out. He peeks from around the side of one barrel and fires a quick succession of four shots into Butler's chest, knocking him back and making him stumble. With the momentary break in fire, the Operator runs to the trash picker's barrier.

"What's this guy's problem?" the young man asks the Operator.

"Beats me," says a nearby voice, the owner hidden behind scrap. "But if they don't stop I'll get out my blaster and start shooting too!"

"Do it!" the Operator says. Lowering his voice, he says, "He's after me. I'll get him to leave you guys alone."

"He thinks he can come into our home and walk out scot-free? Not if we have anything to say about it!" The young man turns to the scrap. "Neil, get your gun out and start shooting!"

"I don't have to listen to you, Rust!"

The Operator looks at the young man at the mention of his name. The trash picker shrugs. "My dad thought it would be funny."

Despite his protest, Neil starts shooting. All the Operator sees is the barrel of a blaster rifle poking through a thick piece of metal. "Go on then!" Neil says before pulling the trigger.

Rust and the Operator run up the stairs while Butler's distracted by the barrage of fire. Once they're on the top level, they turn around and see Butler start up the stairs as well, one hand on each railing.

"Neil's prolly ran," Rust says. "He'll be setting up in a new position soon, you watch."

"Thanks for the help," the Operator says.

Rust looks flabbergasted. "Thanks? We're not done yet!" He grabs the Operator's hand. "Come on!" Together, they scramble up a pile of metal, crawl through the narrow space at the top, and plop down into a corridor left open between the barrier and the wall. There's a popped ball and dolls on the ground. From

MARCOS ANTONIO HERNANDEZ

the nearby store, unseen before because of the scrap metal, a young girl and boy peek out.

"Shh," Rust says, holding his finger up to his mouth before waving them back inside.

A moment later, a heavyset balding man slides in from the other side. "This is Neil," Rust says.

"Howdy," Neil says to the Operator.

The Operator nods.

Rust focuses on a small hole in the wall, waiting. "Now, when I say so, push with all you got," he whispers.

Their heavy breathing and Butler's muffled steps are all the Operator hears.

"Three . . . two . . . one . . . now!"

The Operator plants his feet and pushes. Neil's climbed so that his back is against the scrap metal barrier and his feet against the mall's wall. Rust adopts Neil's positioning as Butler's booming shots land in the barrier at their back.

The wall collapses on Butler, pinning him beneath. "That'll teach him," Rust says to Neil before giving him a high five. He turns to the Operator. "You get everything you need?"

The Operator taps his pocket. "Have it right here. Are you sure you don't want payment?"

"No way. Thanks to you, this was the best morning I've had in a long time!"

CHAPTER NINETEEN

THE ELEVATOR GOING to Pavlova's room has numbered buttons for the first, second, and third floors, despite the building extending high into the sky. The highest button says SC.

"Security checkpoint?" the Operator says to the concierge android. They're alone on the elevator.

"Yes. From there, another elevator goes up to the tenth. There are two elevator shafts that alternate providing access all the way up to the hundredth."

The Operator looks at the locked square door in the ceiling, imagining accessing the upper levels by climbing through the elevator shaft.

"It's been tried before. I wouldn't recommend it," the concierge android says after following the Operator's gaze.

The elevator dings as they arrive on the third level.

Their destination is the last room in the hall. Every other room starts with the number three; their destination has a simple P.

"Here we are," the concierge android says. His voice rises in pitch at the end of his announcement but it doesn't sound natural, a weak attempt at programmed excitement. The android opens the door, the Operator walks in alone, and the android closes the door behind him.

Pavlova's room is on the corner, with two transparent walls looking out onto the city. Above the glass, jutting out from the building, are multiple reclaimers, square metal machines with vents on all sides. The haze thins out as it's pulled into the reclaimers, and the advertisements on the three buildings on the opposite sides of the intersection spill multicolored neon light into the room. There's a pair of overstuffed tan chairs and a matching sofa in front of a television—all of it surrounded by the windows—and the kitchen near the front door has an island with a marble countertop.

It's the nicest room the Operator's been in since he left the upper levels all those years ago.

Gabi's asleep on the sofa, and Miguel's seated on a stool in front of the window, drinking from a steaming mug and looking at the city beyond.

"I'm pretty sure these are one-way," Miguel says, his voice one notch above a whisper. "I tried waving to someone in another building and they didn't see me."

"Seeing people through the haze is difficult from the upper levels. It just looks clear to us because we're used to it," the Operator says.

"They were on the third level, like us," Miguel says, forlorn. He stands up and walks over to the kitchen to where the Operator stands. Leaning on the counter, he says, "This guy's loaded."

"Agreed," the Operator says. Given the chance, Regulo Pavlova might trade his wealth below the reclaimers for a life on the higher levels, if he were fine losing whatever power he has.

"Did you find ammo for the gun?" Miguel asks.

The Operator empties his pockets onto the black marble and places the revolver next to the bullets. "It wasn't easy," he says before launching into the tale of everything that happened in the abandoned mall.

"So that's where you went," Miguel says when the Operator finishes. "I can't believe Butler tracked you down."

"We were making a lot of noise," the Operator admits.

"But in *Sigma*. I didn't think they'd keep following us over here."

"The districts don't matter above the third," the Operator replies. "If Dr. Howl works for the government, he can travel between the districts without worry. It's the same way people can travel down levels if they want, but going up requires going through security."

"I always forget they don't have districts up there," Miguel says, looking out the window at the building on the opposite side of the intersection. Turning back to the Operator, he says, "Someone came by when you were gone."

"The procurement officer?"

"Not sure—he never said his name. Knocked on the door in the middle of the night, woke both of us up," Miguel says, pointing with his thumb at the sleeping Gabi. "I didn't let them in."

"He wasn't alone?"

"Concierge was with him. I told them to come back when you were here."

The Operator nods.

"She fell right back asleep. I've been up since then, thinking."

"About?"

Miguel pauses for a moment before speaking. "Why don't you take Gabi with you and leave the city? They're never going to stop looking for her, now that they know what she's capable of."

The Operator shakes his head. "That's not a good idea."

"Why not?"

"For one, I've got no idea where I'm going. All I know is I can't stay here. I never wanted to come back at all, but Druid asked me to—I think it was so I could find her and protect her."

"And the best way to protect her would be getting her out of the city, away from Dr. Howl and his creation."

The Operator shakes his head. "I don't want to be responsible for anyone but myself. Bad things happen to people when I'm around. Fenix died, your pool hall got destroyed—it's only dumb luck you weren't taken by the doctor."

"I invited you to stay, remember? And Fenix chose you to be his human. What you do doesn't matter as much as you think it does. There's something called free will."

"And it's my free will to leave the city, alone, once my debt's paid."

"Do you think you'll ever be even? They're going to keep searching, for you and for her."

"We're so close to finding the android refugee camp and you want to give up the search now? The information we need will be knocking on our door soon, and then we'll be done."

"And you'll be free to leave."

"Exactly."

Miguel shakes his head. "Look, amigo, I know there's no point in asking you to stay in Gamma because of me. I'll miss you, there's no doubt about that. But this little girl needs more than a group of androids to raise her! She needs guidance, someone she trusts."

The Operator places his hands on the counter and leans forward. "I'm an android," he says, staring at Miguel. "Or did you forget?"

"I didn't forget," Miguel says, ashamed. "I just think it's time you let someone in."

"I let someone in once. And I left when I found out she was an android, not knowing I was one too."

It's the Operator's turn to look out into the city.

"You can't keep running," Miguel says.

"Watch me."

The Operator walks over to the overstuffed chairs, turns one around, and stares out the window. The few hovercrafts near the reclaimers are older models, with missing paint, numerous scuffs, and bumpers looking like they could fall off at any moment.

Miguel sits in the other overstuffed chair, facing the other direction, and doesn't say a word.

A knock at the door breaks the silence. Gabi turns over in her sleep, readjusting the blanket around her.

"I'll get it," Miguel says. He stands up, walks over to the door, and opens it.

"Is he back?" a man's voice asks. The Operator's heard the voice before—his hand goes down to his holster as his head turns around.

"He is. Come in," Miguel says, opening the door and allowing the man inside. The concierge android follows.

Nacho stops short when he sees the Operator stand up. "What the hell are you doing here?" he says, his eyes wide. His face becomes even paler behind his red beard.

"Shh. She's sleeping," the Operator says, pointing to Gabi.

"You two know each other?" Miguel asks.

"We've met before," the Operator says.

Nacho lifts the stub at the end of his right arm from his pocket and shows it to Miguel. "Who do you think did this?"

Miguel looks at the Operator and smiles.

"I didn't know you called yourself the 'procurement officer.' Seems like you know a lot about what goes on in the city," the Operator says to Nacho.

"It's my job." Nacho points his stub, covered in a formfitting black rubber, at Gabi on the couch before becoming self-conscious and putting it back in his pocket. "That the girl you were looking for?"

The Operator looks at the concierge android. "Step outside," he commands.

"I have orders to record this conversation," the concierge says.

Nacho flashes a malicious grin. "If it makes you feel any better, it doesn't matter if he's here or not. The walls are listening."

Miguel gives the Operator a look of concern. They both know he talked about the android refugee camp during their conversation—there's no point in hiding their ultimate destination from the android.

"Pavlova appreciates information almost as much as me," Nacho says, raising his eyebrows. "Now, what do you want?"

"I need to know—we need to know where to find the android refugee hideout," the Operator says.

Nacho's head tilts sideways. "Why? Are you three . . ."

"I am, they're not," the Operator says, hoping an android in their ranks will gain Nacho's trust. A fellow android, searching for more like them.

"I knew it! The way you shot those security 'droids, I said to myself, 'Nacho, that guy's not human!'"

Gabi sits up with a groan. When she realizes they aren't alone, she looks at Nacho with wide eyes. Then she meets Miguel's gaze and gives him a slight nod.

"And now we need to find the camp."

"Someone after you?" Nacho says, concerned. Their shared android experience has created a quick bond.

"Well, the Dominguez brothers, for one," the Operator says, thinking back to the rockets the pair fired at him.

"Don't worry about them, I'll tell them to back off," Nacho says, waving his hand.

For some reason, the Operator believes him. "And, the bigger problem: someone's after her," the Operator says, pointing to Gabi. "Have you heard of Dr. Howl?"

"Heard of him? He's the biggest threat to the camp there is! Him and his ogre Butler. Cass would help you just to spite him, even if you weren't an android."

"Cass?"

"Cassidy Ravensworth. She's in charge of the camp."

"Great. So where can I find it?"

Nacho beckons for Miguel and the Operator to join him at the counter. There, he leans over and uses his finger to outline directions.

"So we're here, right . . ." he begins. Over the next few minutes, he explains how there's a point where all three districts meet, and below that is a water treatment facility.

"It's underground," he says. "And massive. The entire city uses it but doesn't know. Someone stuck Cass there a long time ago, put her in charge of running the place. Whoever it was must've forgot, and didn't tell anyone, because no human's been down there for decades."

CHAPTER TWENTY

Traveling to where the three districts meet requires backtracking at an angle, aboveground, in the direction of the healer's crossing point into Theta. Few people occupy Sigma's streets until they get closer to the specified location. There, children on the street and clotheslines hanging across alleys provide proof of the residents who live far from the district's center. Their shared sense of community becomes apparent when the children huddle in a group and stare at the trio walking through, their parents yelling for them to return home when they spot the strangers for themselves.

The Operator walks in the middle of the street, shielding Miguel and Gabi from a group of adult men gathered on the left side. The children playing on their right keep a close watch on both groups as if they're expecting a showdown.

Miguel nudges the Operator with his elbow after they pass. "Gabi says some of them are androids," he whispers.

The Operator nods once. Androids and humans, living together. They don't look like the surface's typical models, but he's not surprised there are some who can pass as humans living near the refugee camp. His group continues on, the stares from the community following them every step of the way.

Miguel's reports about the presence of androids get more frequent as they get closer to the barrier blocking their path, where Sigma intersects with Theta. He stops whispering after a time—favoring simple nudges—until he reports that everyone looking out into the street, both children and adult alike, are androids, according to Gabi.

"Why do so many live outside the camp?" the Operator whispers to Miguel.

"Maybe they're not allowed in?"

While the Operator thinks about what might happen if they're not allowed in themselves, a pair of men wearing khaki jumpsuits and black face masks—no black hats—turn the corner ahead of them. The Operator looks past Miguel and down at Gabi, who returns his gaze and shakes her head no.

Human security guards, walking through android territory, their beady eyes searching every face.

The Operator avoids looking at them, wondering if Ludavico's brother alerted the rest of his comrades about him. The two guards inspect him and his companions.

Both parties walk by each other without breaking their strides.

Nacho had told them to look for an underground parking garage off the main street. "The entrance is in there, behind a large door," he had said.

They find the specified side street running parallel to the blockade and turn onto it. There's a group of four old men sitting in white plastic chairs across from the gaping hole in the building where cars once drove through in search of parking in the distant past. The end of the road is blocked by a scrap metal barrier; on the far side lies Gamma. Gabi repositions herself and walks between Miguel and the Operator. She tugs on the Operator's arm, pulling him down. "They all are," she whispers in his ear.

The Operator nods and returns to standing. To him, none of them seem armed. But he could deal with them if they are, as long as they aren't as modified as Butler.

There's something reassuring about more androids near the refugee camp. It's as if everyone who doesn't quite belong anyplace in the city can come to this haven and live in peace—or in peace's shadow.

A steep ramp descends from street level down into the parking garage. All four gate arms, offset in pairs of two, are gone, splintered near their attachment points. The windows of the attendant's booth are cloudy with spots of black mold creeping up from the bottom and lining the interior.

The parking garage is the same distance below the surface as the midline. Rows of cars extend into the shadows beyond the reach of the few overhead lights still left on, all of their tires flat or missing and sitting on their rims.

"I've never seen so many still intact," Miguel says in awe. "This is what people used to travel in before everyone switched to hovercrafts," he says to Gabi.

"Before the vertical revolution," the Operator adds.

Gabi rolls her eyes. The Operator and Miguel look at each other and chuckle.

"Nacho said there's a huge door," the Operator says. "Maybe at the end of the lights?"

The trio walks deeper into the parking garage. At some point, Gabi reaches up and holds Miguel's hand while she looks into the shadows behind each car. She stares into the darkness when they walk by the center of another aisle.

"There's androids back there," she says.

Miguel looks in the direction of her gaze. "I don't see anything," he says.

"I can see their glow," she adds.

"There's probably some sleeping back there," the Operator says. Something about being close to an android safe haven brings a sense of well-being, and he's certain other androids who feel the same way would choose sleeping nearby instead of going to the surface or beyond.

The illuminated area ends at another descending ramp. There's nothing distinguishing about the wall ahead of them, other than that the cars parked nearby are missing their exterior paneling.

"Where are all the rats?" Miguel asks. "Haven't seen one down here yet."

"They're probably in the shadows," the Operator says. "Or around those androids Gabi saw."

The Operator looks around. "See anywhere that could be the entrance? There's that normal door over there," he says, pointing to the door near the ramp on their right. "But Nacho said it was 'huge.' I don't see any huge doors."

"Maybe he meant it was important," Miguel says. He pulls himself away from Gabi's grip and tries the access door. "It's just a concrete staircase," he reports. "Should we go down another level?"

"Nacho only mentioned going down the ramp once," the Operator says. "Maybe it's in the shadows? The lights could be to throw people off from finding it."

"Maybe the androids Gabi saw could tell us," Miguel says.

"Or they're guarding the entrance," the Operator adds, thinking out loud.

"Of course they are! Don't know why we didn't realize that before. Come on," Miguel says, taking Gabi's hand and leading the way.

They get to the aisle where Gabi reported the glow. Before they plunge into the shadows, Gabi pulls her hand away from Miguel and starts backing up.

"They're closer," she says.

"Come on, we're almost there," Miguel says, reaching for her hand.

Gabi turns and runs back towards the ramp leading up to the surface. The Operator and Miguel are both about to chase after her but they're stopped in their tracks by the sight of a towering, long-haired man in a black trench coat turning the corner at the bottom of the ramp.

Butler lifts the guns attached to the ends of both arms. Gabi's frozen—he aims above and past her.

At the same moment, the Operator pulls Miguel behind the closest car, opposite the dark aisle. Butler's booming shots send loud echoes through the confined space. Right after, a volley of shots erupts from where Gabi saw the androids in the shadows, on the Operator's flank, forcing him and Miguel to find refuge between the front of the car and the parking garage wall. Small holes in the concrete wall appear, accompanied by chalky dust.

Through the adjacent car's window, the Operator, his gun in hand, sees Gabi with her hands over both ears and her chin tucked. Dr. Howl's head appears from around the corner behind Butler, and he smiles when he sees Gabi alone in the middle of the illuminated area. Behind Dr. Howl comes a stream of androids in gray compression suits, each with a blaster rifle held to their shoulder.

Miguel pulls out his gun and holds it against his chest with both hands, the barrel towards the ceiling.

Butler, having seen where the Operator and Miguel hid, marches forward, shooting against the sides of the car between them. Gabi flinches with each shot.

"Don't just stand there, shoot at the car!" Dr. Howl

commands the android reinforcements. Then, he yells to Butler, "Ignore them, grab the girl!"

Without hesitation, Butler leans over and wraps both arms around Gabi. He turns and walks away with his cargo. The Operator tries aiming through the glass of the cars between them but no effective angle exists—he leans left and right, always aware of both groups of firing androids. Miguel, caught up in the moment, stands up and fires his revolver while exposing himself to fire from his flank. His shot hits Butler in the back. The two-gunned android stumbles forward and Gabi slithers away while the Operator pulls Miguel back into cover.

"I'm fine, I'm fine," Miguel says. "Did you see I hit him!"

The Operator watches as Gabi tries running away. She doesn't get more than a few steps before one of the androids in gray compression grabs her and retreats behind a wall of his comrades.

Butler, with the girl now in Dr. Howl's custody, turns and glares at the Operator and Miguel's hiding place. With a roar, he resumes his march towards their hideout.

"We've got to go," the Operator says to Miguel, grabbing his shoulder. A shot from the androids at their flank hits the wall— the attackers have stepped into the light. With four well-placed shots from the Operator, four headless androids fall to the ground in a flurry of sparks.

"No!" Miguel says, ripping himself away. He tries standing up, but the Operator pulls him back down. "We'll get her back. I promise."

"I can't just leave her like you're planning to leave us!" Miguel yells, trying to stand up once more. "Let go of me," he says, squirming and exhausted.

The Operator puts his hands over Miguel ears, forcing his friend to look him in the face. "We'll get her back. I promise."

Miguel flexes his jaw.

The gunfire against the side of the car reminds them of the danger. Miguel nods. Both he and the Operator maneuver between the front bumpers and the wall of the row of cars, crouching as Butler's shots hit all around them.

CHAPTER TWENTY-ONE

THE OPERATOR DRAGS Miguel across the open space between the last car in the row and the stairway access door on the far wall. His friend's legs offer little help besides the occasional push against the ground, and by the time the Operator slams the door open and drags the two of them through he's almost carrying the man.

"I'm light-headed," Miguel says as the Operator closes the door behind them. Butler's booming shots continue from beyond the door, slamming into the metal and filling the stairwell with noise.

The Operator lays Miguel down on the ground and spots a dark stain on his brown button-down shirt. Lifting the bottom, he discovers blood seeping into the waist of his jeans. There's a hole on his right side, just above the hip, and an exit wound on his lower back.

"You were shot," the Operator says in disbelief.

"Must have been from the ones in the shadows," Miguel says with a cough. He winces from the pain. "I didn't feel it."

"Come on," the Operator says, grabbing Miguel's left hand and making him sit up. He leans over and puts his neck into

Miguel's armpit before standing. A groaning Miguel offers what little help he can.

With Miguel in a fireman's carry, the Operator walks down the stairs with Butler's shots still hitting the metal door behind them. He exits the stairwell at the level below, walking into the darkness of the parking garage's lower level. Car-sized wells of darkness stand out in the shadows from rows upon rows of abandoned, useless vehicles.

The Operator walks as far as he can away from the stairs before sitting Miguel down behind a car. He pulls his blaster out and rests his arms against the trunk of a sedan, aimed in the rough direction of the door they came through.

At some point, the shooting stopped. The lone sounds in the space are the Operator's heavy breathing and Miguel's whimpers of pain. The Operator waits for Butler, expecting a loud crash of the metal door against the wall when it's thrown open with too much force. Or, in the absence of the aggressive entrance, his heavy footsteps. At the very least, the androids spilling down the stairs or coming from the ramp cars once took between the above floor and his current location.

When nothing happens, the Operator holsters his blaster and turns his attention to Miguel. "Nacho set us up," he says.

"You think so?"

"How else did they find us? They knew *exactly* where we were. I doubt the android refugee camp is even here."

"They have Gabi," Miguel whispers.

"I know. We'll get her back," the Operator says. "Don't worry about her. Focus on your breathing."

"I'm trying, but I'm getting so tired."

The Operator puts his right hand behind Miguel's head and taps his friend's face with his left. "Keep your eyes open. You've got to stay awake."

"Just a quick nap."

The Operator touches Miguel's shirt, feeling for the extent of the dampness. The blood has seeped into the shirt near his chest. He makes Miguel sit up, leaning him against the car.

"I'm going for help," the Operator says. "Someone outside the parking garage has to know a healer nearby." He stands up, then bends back down and lifts Miguel's chin in the darkness. "Stay awake, help will be here soon."

Not wanting to go back through the staircase in case someone's waiting for him on the other side of the door, the Operator walks back to the level above using the ramp. With his blaster in hand, ready to shoot his way through the masses for his friend's sake, he stays close to the wall, his eyes scanning the low-light environment for androids ahead or looking down from over the barrier above. He finds no threats, and peers over the car closest to the ramp before emerging onto the scene of the shoot-out.

There's nobody waiting for him. On the ground, within the overhead light's reach, are the androids that Gabi saw, now headless. He's glad the androids who flanked them and shot Miguel were left behind—it's a fitting fate for their attackers. Wary of more androids lurking in the shadows where Gabi first saw the others, the Operator uses the cars past which he made his escape with Miguel as cover, going all the way to the corner where he first saw Butler.

There's no evidence Dr. Howl, Butler, and the reinforcement androids were ever there.

The Operator hurries from behind the protection of the cars, in case there are enemies hidden in the shadows, and walks with his back against the left-side ramp wall, alternating looking both directions.

The androids that were sitting on the street opposite the ramp's entrance are no longer there. The white plastic chairs they sat on are empty—nobody lingers behind after Dr. Howl and company showed up.

Walking back towards the center of Sigma, the Operator's stunned nobody is in the streets. All the children are missing. The parents watching them, gone. An entire community disappeared in a brief sliver of time.

He walks through the center of the street, looking for signs of life. Even the clotheslines are gone, withdrawn into the surrounding buildings. Looking down an alley, he discovers a flash of movement—a rat, strolling between buildings without a care in the world.

"Hello?" the Operator says, daring the noise. He's convinced Dr. Howl and everyone the man brought is long gone, and wonders what occurred to inspire the level of fear that led to the surrounding androids disappearing.

The Operator looks up, past the reclaimers. The buildings don't have any of the typical flashing neon billboards. Instead, the exteriors are lined with the cargo containers hoverbarges carry throughout the city, with more hoverbarges moving between the constricted lanes—an industrial area, the traffic slow-moving. He spots a flash of sleek purple typical of the reinforcement carrier through the numerous wide crafts above him, but when he looks for the vehicle again he can't find it.

Knocking on a door where he saw a mother yell for her child to come back home when she saw the Operator, Miguel, and Gabi, he discovers a broken lock. The door swings open and he finds a room filled with dust and debris—it's clear nobody's lived inside for years. Footprints in the rubble end just inside the door, like the mother never bothered leaving the entrance's vicinity.

Any hope of finding someone who can help Miguel dissolves in an instant, replaced by dread. Nothing's right in this now-abandoned part of the city, and the Operator can't shake the feeling he has missed a crucial something staring him right in the face. He turns and looks at the surrounding buildings that were teeming with life and community minutes before and loses his sense of gravity. It's as if he's falling, even though he's standing straight up.

The Operator turns and runs back to the parking garage, his blaster in hand. He turns the corner onto the street with the plastic chairs sitting in front and shoots one on a whim, knocking it over, before running down the ramp. There's no hesitation about running in front of the shadowed areas in the parking garage anymore, nor worry about hidden androids. Somehow, he knows he's alone in this part of the city. He and Miguel, his friend lying alone behind a car in the darkness below.

The Operator leaves the illuminated area and runs down the second ramp, descending to the second level below the surface. Depths the midliners favor.

"Miguel?" he says out loud. His voice echoes off the walls. "Miguel!"

With a sense of the stairwell door's location, he feels along the wall until he finds it. Then he retraces the steps he took with his friend on his back, all the while calling out his friend's name, worried his friend went to sleep and won't be waking up.

He gets to the car where he thinks he left Miguel and crouches down, his hands searching in the darkness as he walks forward. When he gets to the vehicle's front tire, he knows his friend isn't there. But he knows he's in the general vicinity.

"Miguel!" he says again, at the top of his lungs, hopeful the sound will wake his friend. The sound echoes throughout the darkness. When it dies out, the Operator pauses, listening for the sound of ragged breathing. There's nothing but the sound of his own body—his breathing and internal fluids pumping throughout. He goes around the front of the car, jumping over the hood because it's parked so close to the wall ahead, and crouches down, feeling for his friend, wary of stepping on him or kicking him. At the rear tire, he gives up on that space, going around the trunk on his way to the next opening between cars.

The Operator goes through a dozen spaces between cars before he begins a different kind of search: feeling the sides of the cars for blood, proof that he hasn't imagined the entire scenario. On the precipice of questioning his entire reality, uncertain if his programming's at fault—if it's been at fault from the very beginning—he searches the spaces again, doubling back on where he passed through. Back where he thought he left Miguel in the first place, where he first searched, he finds a wet spot on the car's exterior.

He stands, grateful he hasn't imagined it all, and wipes his hands on his pants. Panic replaces his gratitude: Where's Miguel? The Operator bends down and puts his hands on the ground, looking for wet spots where his friend might have crawled away, if he had somehow returned to consciousness despite the loss of blood.

There are no wet spots on the ground. Miguel has disappeared, along with everyone else in this part of the city, in the span of time the Operator climbed the ramp to the illuminated level above.

With no reason for staying in the darkness, the Operator walks back up the ramp to the level where the shooting occurred. He kicks the closest car, cursing Nacho's name, certain that the next time he finds the man he'll shoot him right between the eyes.

The large wall at the end of the illuminated portion of the parking garage draws his attention. "Can't miss it," Nacho had said about the entrance to the camp, claiming it was a "huge door." The Operator notices a line running vertical down the center of the concrete. He's not sure if it was there before, but then again, he's not sure of anything after discovering the disappearance of an entire community.

Placing his ear against the wall, the Operator thinks he hears the sound of distant running water. He tries squeezing the middle three fingers of each hand into the seam, palms away from each other, and when he tries pulling the wall apart his fingers slip and fingernails rip from the skin.

Seeing his own body fluids provides a release he didn't expect. With a frantic energy fueled by his own pain, he places all six of the same fingers onto one side of the seam and leans to the right, pulling with everything he has.

The concrete wall budges with a groan.

CHAPTER TWENTY-TWO

THE OPERATOR STANDS BACK from the wall, stunned at the movement. He licks the blood from his fingers one at a time and wipes them on his pants. After taking a large gulp of air, he inserts eight digits into the wider opening, getting as much surface area as he can onto one side, and starts pulling. Consistent pulling doesn't produce movement, but yanking opens the concrete slab a bit farther each time. Behind the split is a second door, made of rusted dark metal.

When the gap in the concrete reaches shoulder width, the Operator puts a hand on each side and tries prying it apart. His chest muscles scream and his fingers ache. Despite the pain, he tucks his chin and sets his jaw, pulling with everything he has. He thinks about Miguel, about Gabi, about Dr. Howl and Butler chasing him down and terrorizing everyone he knows.

All of a sudden, the concrete slab begins moving on its own, accompanied by the sound of grinding gears. It stops at the width of a car, at which point the metal door beyond begins opening.

A long concrete hallway, with a light gray cement floor that matches the parking garage's, becomes visible beyond, lit by a series of white light boxes along the left wall, just below the ceiling. The metal door stops when it matches the width of the concrete slab's opening. Then, a skinless android head, dull gray metal, appears from behind the right side. It reminds the Operator of the concierge android.

"Hello," the android says. The voice could belong to a human female. They inspect the space around the Operator. "Come in," they say, beckoning with a skinless metal hand. Four fingers end in delicate points—the fifth, the index finger, is missing its top half.

As soon as the Operator walks through the two doors, the android pushes a button. The concrete slabs close with a loud thud, then the metal door closes, a hiss emanating from somewhere behind the button before the doors come together with a delicate touch.

A white plastic chair, identical to the ones outside the parking garage's entrance, is next to the button. The android sits back down and tells the Operator he can go on ahead.

"Ahead?" the Operator asks.

"To the camp. That's why you were prying the doors apart, right?"

The Operator's elation about finding the camp dies when he realizes there's no longer any point. He doesn't have Gabi, he's lost Miguel, and his fingers are bloodied.

Before the Operator can ask the android guarding the entrance any questions, they tuck their chin and become inert.

Alone, the Operator realizes there's a consistent groan from machines accompanying the sound of rushing water coming at him from the end of the hall. It drowns out his footsteps as he walks. The hall ends at a concrete wall and is longer than it first appeared—it reminds the Operator of walking into the shadows of the midline, unsure of what lies waiting for him at the end.

There's a square opening on the right wall at the hall's end.

Cool air rushes past his face as he approaches, adding more noise to the faraway whir of machines. Walking through, the Operator finds himself on the top level of an open rectangular chasm, in one of its uppermost corners. Balconies surround each level all the way down. At the bottom, with dozens of balconies below him, are a series of massive machines, each one a half circle, dwarfing the few people walking around them. His eyes water from the air flying at his face. Looking up, he finds a massive vent situated in the middle of the rectangular ceiling above.

Taking a look at his more local surroundings, the Operator realizes that every balcony is made of different materials. Some are rusted metal, some made from a mixture of plastics, and others no more than fabric pulled taut against hidden supports. Where he stands and the nearby staircase are made from industrial black metal—the rest of the balconies branch out from the staircase's various landings. There are no doors beyond the balconies; the walls are solid concrete. A cluster of people lie still on the balcony just below him on the adjacent wall. Looking closer onto each space he can see from his vantage point, he realizes there are dozens of unmoving people throughout the makeshift habitats hanging from the walls.

"They're in standby mode," a woman's voice says from behind the Operator. Startled, he turns around, his hand hovering over his blaster.

"They won't be much longer. Everyone's been waiting for the androids outside to leave."

The Operator stares at the woman. She's wearing her brown hair up, with a folded bandana tied around her head. Her large brown eyes would draw any man's attention, human or android, and her thick, greasy hands don't look like they belong on her petite frame.

"I'm sorry, you don't know who I am. I'm Cass, in charge of the water treatment since day one," she says, holding her hand out.

The Operator shakes it. "It's nice to meet you."

"And you are?"

"Just passing through."

Cass laughs. "Well, we have you to thank for getting rid of everyone outside the camp," she says.

"How do you know?"

"Cameras," she says, pointing to a small hole in the concrete above the entrance to the hallway. Unrecognizable, without knowing it's there.

"We don't get many visitors, and now we've got two just minutes apart," she says, tilting her head to the side in a beckoning gesture and walking away.

Miguel. The Operator follows, eager for information. "Wait, was the other guy injured?" he says.

"He was. Is. We went out and got him when the coast was clear. The people outside were living there for months, waiting for us to come out."

"Where is he?"

"In the infirmary. We're going there now. We can take care of those fingers too," she says, pointing with her chin at the Operator's hands.

Cass starts walking down the staircase.

"Wait, how did you survive if you couldn't leave?"

"There are other ways in and out," Cass says with a wink. "Only essentials were allowed to leave; they brought back supplies for the rest of us."

"Weren't they worried about the water supply?" the Operator asks.

"That's why they brought so many androids with them and

made them wait outside. Those were the ones that were going to take over caring for the machines."

"And now they're gone."

"Thanks to you."

"Are you worried they'll come back?"

"Somewhat, but we'll deal with that when the time comes. If it's not that, some other problem will show up that we'll have to deal with."

The Operator tries putting a hand on the railing during their walk down but pulls away when he realizes he's left blood on the surface. He pauses and wipes it with the sleeve of his shirt.

The machines on the bottom level rise higher from the ground than the level of the reclaimers on the surface. Each one is gleaming metal, their consistent whirring evidence of their proper care. There's rushing water in the background, far below the machines. As the machines whir away nonstop, people move between multiple rooms branching off into the same walls that hold people in hanging habitats high above them.

There's a large cafeteria where both human-looking and skinless androids share tables. A break room has multiple couches and cushioned chairs, each one occupied.

"The infirmary's over here," Cass says, continuing on.

"Is everyone—" the Operator begins.

"An android? Yes. Mostly."

The Operator doesn't inquire further.

The infirmary is two small rooms, and the lone area possessing a door. Inside, Cass explains that it was made for humans before they decided androids were a better option for dealing with the continuous labor. "We've still got all the supplies from the initial construction," she says.

A second door opens and a skinless android comes out.

Beyond the door, Miguel lies on a hospital bed with a white blanket up to his chin.

The android is shorter than every other specimen they've walked by, and when made to look human there's a good chance they'd be a child.

"He's lost a lot of blood," the medical android says, in a female voice.

"She helped a doctor above the surface before she came down here," Cass explains. "The best we have."

"Will he live?" the Operator asks.

"I don't know."

"Can I see him?"

The medical android looks at the Operator. He hangs his head when he realizes how long it's been since he's had a change of clothes, or made any attempts at cleaning himself up.

"It's probably not a good idea," the Operator says.

"Agreed. Let me take a look at your hands," the medical android says.

The Operator holds them out. After inspection, the android mutters while she shuffles through a nearby drawer. She pulls out a clear barrel syringe with a black plunger and doesn't attach a needle. Taking the Operator's hands, she squeezes a clear viscous fluid on the tip of each finger. Within seconds, the fluid color matches the Operator's skin and any extra absorbs, leaving behind fingers that look like they've never been damaged.

"That stuff's like magic," the Operator says, flexing his fingers.

"It's what we use on the water treatment machines. We always make sure we have it on hand," Cass explains, waiting. The short android lets out a juvenile giggle when she under-stands the joke, and the Operator thinks for a moment before he laughs as well.

"One of the things that works on both humans and androids," the medical android says.

"What would it do if you put it on your finger?" the Operator asks. Without skin, all of her body's fluids are within her skeleton.

"Looks like metal but doesn't harden," the medical android says. "Keeps the fluids in though."

"Were you skinless on the surface?" the Operator asks.

Cass hits the Operator in the upper arm with the back of her hand.

"What?" he says.

"It's all right," the medical android says. "No, I fit in up there. And now, I fit in down here—we're all androids."

"Don't go around asking that," Cass warns him.

"What if you wanted to fit in again?"

"If I wanted to re-skin? I'd have to take someone's. It happens sometimes, when other specialties are needed on the surface."

"Let's go," Cass says, pulling the Operator's arm.

"I'll let you know if anything happens with your friend!" the medical android calls out as they leave.

Cass turns on the Operator when they're back in the main room. "Down here, we respect everyone's decisions about their own bodies. Stay out of their business." The sternness in her voice leaves no room for debate.

"Done. Now I need something from you," the Operator says. He tells Cass all about Gabi, about being chased by Dr. Howl and Butler, and the events that led to them being in the parking garage. Cass curses when she hears Nacho's name.

"He wouldn't lift a finger for us when he was down here," she says, shaking her head.

"That doesn't surprise me."

"Though that was a long time ago." A moment later, she says, "Butler took the girl."

The Operator looks at her, surprised.

"Cameras," she says, pointing to another small hole above the lounge.

"He did. And I need your help getting her back."

CHAPTER TWENTY-THREE

"I'D GIVE it to you if we had it, but the upper levels just shut down our distribution center. They took our whole reserve supply," Klepsydra says, annoyed.

The Operator, now back in Gamma, stands on the stage while the rest of the White Jackets sit around their table.

"Why do you need so much? No way it's just for you," the White Jackets' leader asks.

"No, I don't even use the stuff." The Operator then tells Klepsydra and her fellow White Jackets how he needs the stuff for Cass, that it's the arrangement they made in exchange for help getting Gabi back from Dr. Howl.

"You're going to *him*? Good luck. But like I said, we don't have any until our next shipment gets here. The workers said a man running from androids gave away the location," she says, tilting her head while looking at the Operator. She blinks twice. Turning away, she says, "I had to have a meeting with the Enforcer above the fourth and everything."

"Are they ever going to send a replacement for Bacas?" the Operator asks.

"They said they're exploring their options."

"I say you lobby for the position yourself," one of the White Jackets says, a young woman with short hair and freckles.

"It's one of the options they're exploring," Klepsydra says.

"Well, where can I get more Stim?" the Operator says.

"Why do androids need Stim anyways? Does it even work on you?"

"It works, just isn't as potent as it is on humans. Still addictive though. Some of them work on the upper levels—don't ask me how they get there—and they use Stim so they can work for a full week at a time before coming back on the weekends."

"Bet they're quite popular with their bosses," the young woman says. After a stern look from Klepsydra, she lowers her gaze and looks at her hands resting on the table.

"We're not due for another shipment until next week—"

"I need it sooner than that," the Operator interjects.

"If you'd let me finish," Klepsydra says, the feathers of the bird tattoo moving when she flexes her neck. "But the upper levels get shipments every few days." She turns to the freckled young woman. "Rose, we still have access to the shipping logs, right?"

Rose, the silenced member, meets Klepsydra's eyes and nods.

"Good. Let's hijack a shipment." Turning back to the Operator, she demands half of whatever they take. "That should be enough to replace what we lost," she says.

"Deal. Cass didn't give me an exact amount, just said to get as much as I could."

"Perfect."

Looking back to Rose, Klepsydra says, "Take him and see if anything's coming soon."

Rose stands up and walks from the room. The Operator follows her into one of the stage's back rooms. A large computer desk with multiple screens and numerous wires hanging down from the ceiling takes up most of the space. Rose sits down in the sole chair and the Operator leans on the wall next to the door.

"Let's see here," Rose says. The monitors come alive after a series of rapid keystrokes. The blue screens are covered with small red text, the displayed symbols crossing from bottom to top while she works.

"And now we're into the shipping logs . . . isolating the chunk of levels just above us . . . and now checking for the closest one to us geographically . . ."

She turns around, triumphant. "There's a shipment set for delivery tonight. The bazaar on the sixth," she tells the Operator.

"Let's get it done," the Operator says, clapping his hands.

A burly White Jacket blocks the path back to the stage for both the Operator and Rose. "Klepsydra said she'd come find you when they're done," he tells them.

Rose grumbles and turns around. The Operator sizes up the man. When Rose realizes the Operator and the guard are staring each other down, she grabs the Operator and pulls him back into the computer room.

The Operator sits on the ground, his back against the wall; Rose, in her chair. "Why do you need all this hardware?" the Operator says.

"Klepsydra likes to know what happens in the levels above Gamma," Rose explains. "You'd be surprised how much the upper level's problems trickle down to us."

"Like what?"

"Like when you gave away all that frozen meat—we saw it on the cameras. We had our shipment reduced because the upper levels needed more."

The Operator squeezes his lips together and nods.

"Or when Dr. Howl went into the badlands. We made sure

everyone was off the streets and closed down the market so he wouldn't give the residents any problems."

"So you're monitoring the city's logistics?"

"You have no idea."

Rose turns around and returns her attention to the screens. The Operator thinks about Gabi, Miguel, and what he's going to do if and when he runs into Butler again. He's wondering if blocking the sewers worked at preventing rats from going below the surface when Klepsydra walks in.

"Did you find anything?"

"Shipment coming in to the bazaar tonight."

"On the sixth? Contact Beezle and tell him to drop a rope from the seventh. What time?"

"Scheduled for seven thirty."

"Just after the sun goes down." Klepsydra looks at the Operator. "Good thing you're wearing mostly black."

The Operator looks at her, confused.

"By the way: you're not getting any help from us."

"What?" the Operator says, standing up.

"You heard me. It's your fault we lost our supply in the first place. This is your chance to earn it back."

She continues when the Operator doesn't respond. "The men can't talk, but they made sure I knew what the man who broke into the distribution center looked like." She points at the Operator, moving her finger in a circle.

Rose pokes her head out from behind Klepsydra. "I'll tell you what to do," she says.

After the sun goes down, Rose and the Operator walk along the streets of Gamma, stopping below the white hoverbarges that jut out from where they're parked on the sixth level at the bazaar. She looks at the watch she put on her wrist before they left. "The rope should be here in three . . . two . . ." She points at the building in front of them, and a black rope falls from above.

The Operator, his hands gloved, steps forward and grabs the rope, giving it a yank. It doesn't budge.

"Wish me luck," he says, putting his feet against the building and supporting all of his weight with his hands.

Climbing to the seventh level is tedious work. Breathing is easier once he's past the reclaimers, but it's accompanied by a mild anxiety about discovery. Hovercrafts zip through the air behind him—he's certain each one will report a strange man climbing to the upper levels. He reorients himself below the fifth level so he travels around a pink flashing billboard, guessing that a moving dark spot on the lights would draw more attention than the dark spot next to it. Going off the vertical axis requires a drastic lean—his shoes slip against the building's glass exterior but never give way.

The Operator climbs until he's higher than the hoverbarges outside the bazaar. Then, he moves horizontally until he's above the one farthest to the right. Letting go of some rope, he lowers himself onto the hoverbarge before releasing the rope altogether.

The wind rushes against the Operator's face as he appreciates the city from his vantage point. The noiseless hovercrafts high above zip through the air, the neon lights from the towering buildings reflecting off their shimmering exteriors. He can see why the upper levels don't worry about the districts below—their differences seem remote, the small concerns of a different world. The buildings extend far into the sky, their highest levels untouchable through limits on flight altitude and from within by stratifications that rely on money and status.

Pulling his attention away from his momentary awe, the Operator runs across the tops of the hoverbarges until he's at the three vacant spaces in the middle. He goes to the end farthest from the building, lies down, and waits.

As expected, the Stim transport is a winged craft the length of the cargo hold he's standing on, and three wide. It descends straight down from above after traveling to the building from somewhere else in the city, staying close to the building but still accommodating the cargo holds. As it drops to the correct level, the Operator is left staring at his own reflection in a one-way black mirror for a brief moment. If they see him, they'll leave.

The transport ship doesn't make any sudden movements. It pauses for a brief moment, preparing for entry into the three spaces left in the row of hoverbarges.

It's the moment the Operator has been waiting for, and he doesn't hesitate. He jumps onto one wing, turning the entire craft on its side with his weight. The vehicle doesn't stray right with the Operator hanging onto a crevice, instead turning on its axis.

"Pilot's not bad," the Operator says. His words evaporate into the night air.

He scrambles up the wing as the craft stabilizes and reaches the main area just as the side door opens, exposing a man in a khaki jumpsuit and black hat. The Operator grabs the man and tosses him out. Then, he climbs into the craft and shuts the door.

A shot hits the wall right past the Operator's head and he ducks behind one of two pallets filled with small boxes. "What kind of idiot robs a government transport?" a man yells from the front.

It's the second man of two, according to Rose. "Don't give them time to call for backup," she had said. The Operator stands while firing two shots—one hits the man in the hand that holds his blaster, the other in the leg.

The guard never fires a second shot.

Running forward, the Operator kicks the man's weapon away and stands over him. "There's no way you'll get away with this," the pilot says.

"Don't worry about me," the Operator replies. He applies

pressure to the man's leg before taking a nearby strap and wrapping it multiple times around the wound, tying it off against a hook on the wall. "You'll be all right—just don't do anything stupid. And keep pressure on your arm."

"Do you know the risk you're taking?" the pilot says.

"There are people below who need this more than you."

The Operator climbs into the pilot's seat. Through the one-way windshield, he sees a confused guard staring at the craft from the open space where they were expecting a landing inside the building, the three partitions that separated the hoverbarges removed.

There's not much time. The Operator puts the transport into a nosedive. The pilot rises up with a yelp.

"Hold that arm," the Operator says without turning around.

With the surface fast approaching, the Operator waits until the last moment before pulling the craft back to level. A swarm of people emerge from the nearby buildings and take every last box from the pallets in seconds. When they're done, the Operator flies the ship back up to the sixth-level bazaar, parking it on top of the hoverbarges. They groan with the added load and end up angled down.

Police sirens ring out from high above as the Operator runs across the top of the hoverbarges. He jumps, grabs the rope, and lets it run between his hands as he falls back to the surface. He tightens his grip once he's past the reclaimers. His shoulders scream with the sudden jolt. The heat in his hands is almost unbearable, but he has no choice but to hold on. He lets his feet hit the side of the building at the first level, sliding down until he's safe on the surface, where Rose waits for him.

She escorts him into a nearby building while he holds his hands in front of his chest.

"You'll be fine," she says, after glancing at the tattered gloves. She smiles. "You just set the record for the fastest heist."

CHAPTER TWENTY-FOUR

Cᴀss ᴛᴀᴘs her foot while she waits with crossed arms for the Operator at the bottom of the stairs in the android refugee camp. "Did you get the Stim?" she asks, the large water treatment machines looming behind her. The rest of the androids in their vicinity make a point of not paying attention to the interaction.

"I did," the Operator says, nodding. "How's Miguel?"

"Still hasn't woken up. Where is it?"

"There's a pallet's worth in the midline on Gamma. All yours."

Cass's eyes widen. "An entire pallet?"

The Operator nods.

"You could've brought some back with you," she laments before turning around and calling an android who could have been a lumberjack in a different environment. When the summoned android walks over, she tells him to get three more people and bring back the Stim.

"Go through the tunnels," she adds. "And hurry, before the midliners get a hold of the stuff."

The Operator walks towards the infirmary, leaving Cass behind. She hurries after him.

"I told you, he's still asleep," she says.

The Operator nods and continues walking. The medical android, eating lunch in the cafeteria, spots him going towards her domain and follows, leaving her food behind.

Miguel hasn't moved while the Operator was gone. There are no chairs in the small room, and the Operator rests his back against the wall and watches his friend's slow, shallow breaths.

"I gave him something to keep him still," the medical android says when she walks into the room. "Can't have him opening the wound by twisting while he sleeps."

"What if he wakes up?" the Operator asks, wondering if Miguel is, in fact, awake but trapped inside his own body.

"I'd imagine he'll be uncomfortable for a while, until the paralysis wears off. He won't ever have more than a few hours though."

"Are you sure about that?"

"Positive."

The Operator turns to Cass. "You got your Stim. Now let's get Gabi back."

Cass turns away. "I've asked around, and there aren't many who are willing to risk their lives for a girl they don't know."

"What do you mean? You can't make them?"

"The camp doesn't work like that. Outside of the mandatory work on the water treatment, everyone's free to do as they please."

The Operator tilts his head back and exhales. "So, I got the Stim for nothing?"

"There are a few always looking for a fight."

"Look, we need to get her back. Not just for me—all of you are in very real danger now that Gabi's in Dr. Howl's hands."

He then tells Cass and the medical android about how Gabi can sense androids, telling them that if Dr. Howl ever replicates the ability there's no chance of androids moving through the above levels undetected. "They'll track us everywhere. The androids already known by them don't have anything to worry about, but all of you, living outside society, will be exposed the second you step out of the camp."

Cass thinks for a moment. "How sure are you of her capabilities?"

"She knew I was an android from the very first time we met."

"You're an android?" Cass and the medical android say in unison. Cass walks forward and pokes his face. The medical android, stunned, says she glued the wounds on his fingers and couldn't tell.

"You must be the most advanced in the camp," Cass says. "Where did you come from?"

"The fifty-second. And Gabi knew right away. No android is safe, they'll hunt us like animals."

"What are you doing way down here?" the medical android says, awestruck.

"It's a long story . . . and it doesn't matter. The point is, we need to get her back before Dr. Howl harnesses her ability and uses it against us."

"How does she do it?"

"I'm not sure. She says it looks like a glow. And she doesn't even need to see the body—she can see the glow through the darkness."

Cass puts her arm on the wall for support. "Okay, this changes the calculations quite a bit."

"We can't afford *not* rescuing her."

"I'm starting to see that. Convincing the others won't be

easy. Give me some time." Cass hurries out of the room, lost in thought.

"Have you eaten?" the medical android asks.

"No. Really though, I just want to sleep. It's been a long day."

"Well, let's get you fed and then I'll show you where you can get some rest."

The Operator acquiesces and follows the medical android to the cafeteria. Workers covered in grease fill every table, some in boisterous groups and others sitting alone. After standing in line and grabbing a plastic tray with a bowl filled with a thick porridge, he sits down next to the medical android as she finishes her interrupted meal.

"Nobody cared about a human looking for a human girl," the medical android says while the Operator eats, her own food gone. "Things will be different now that we know you're one of us."

The Operator grunts and downs another bite.

"The humans in the upper levels will be surprised at how many androids there really are among them," she says. "I don't know if they'll even believe some of the ones they discover."

"What do you mean?"

"That glue? You know how it works on both humans and androids? Well, it also works *between* humans and androids."

The Operator sets his spoon down. He folds his hands and rests his elbows on the table. "I'm not following," he says.

"Well, jobs aren't always available for androids. So, some of the people in the camp take a human's job."

"That was their fear when androids showed up in the first place."

"Yes, but not exactly." The medical android looks around and makes sure nobody's listening. Then, she leans in. "They take their job by taking their identity."

"Taking their identity? Who makes a copy of their face?"

"There's no copy. They take their skin, and we get rid of the body down here."

The Operator stares at the medical android, waiting for the punch line. None comes.

"More like we put it in the midline and it disappears. The midliners do anything for meat."

The Operator takes another bite of porridge, forcing it down his throat despite his disgust. "How often does that happen?" he says after he swallows.

"Almost everyone working on the upper levels has a stolen identity."

"So, a stolen face."

"Yes, if that's how you want to think of it. And they're all in danger if the upper levels can detect unregistered androids."

"That should light a fire under some of their asses."

"You'd think, but there aren't many in the camp at the moment. They're in the upper levels, working long hours boosted by Stim. Some come down here and trade off with another android, but not many. Although . . ."

"What?"

"The resources are shared by the camp. If upper-level employment suffers, everyone suffers. I hope that's how Cass frames it when she asks for help."

The Operator finishes his meal and asks the medical android to show him where he can sleep. She leads him up the first flight of stairs and they walk along a makeshift balcony going over the cafeteria, ending up on a series of steel beams attached to the wall above the infirmary. She points to a bed perched on the beams before walking away, and the Operator collapses atop the blankets, falling asleep within seconds.

He wakes up to Cass yelling from below for him to wake up.

MARCOS ANTONIO HERNANDEZ

"Get down here," she says when he peeks past the bed's edge.

With a groan, the Operator rolls over and swings his legs off the side of the bed. He stands up, and Cass starts walking towards the staircase. Instead of walking along the makeshift balcony, he jumps down from above the infirmary and harnesses his momentum with a roll before standing up.

Cass turns around and grins. "Don't waste any time, do you?"

"What's going on? Is everyone ready to go?" the Operator asks.

"Not exactly. And where would we go? We don't know where Gabi's being held."

Confused, the Operator says he assumed they'd go to Dr. Howl's office.

"Ah yes, right into the government facility and ask for the girl back? We're looking for her, but it's going to take some time."

"Then what do you want?"

"I thought we could take a walk," Cass says, walking away with her arms behind her back.

The Operator sighs and follows.

"How much do you know about Dr. Howl?" she asks.

"Not much, other than he's a scientist with a thing for enhancing androids."

"He does. Always surrounded by androids, all of them following his every command."

"What about it? They work for him."

"They do—he controls their every move. And he hates them."

"Hates them? How do you know?"

Cass turns left, leading them around the last machine in the

168

row. "Because he hates all androids. That's why he stationed surveillance outside our camp, looking for us."

"But why does he hate androids in the first place?"

"Because his mother left his father when she fell in love with an android. They came down here."

"Dr. Howl's mother is *here*?" the Operator says, looking at the numerous balconies attached to the concrete walls above, wondering which one she's in.

"*Was* here. She passed away a few years ago. Not sure if Howl even knows. Anyways, Julian's dad then died by suicide; his death seeded hatred against androids in Julian. Now, he treats them as no more than machines, ignoring advanced cognition—which is why he experiments with the enhancements in the first place. His most popular? Complete control. It's mandatory and present in every security program, so the androids ignore threats to their own existence despite advanced versions' initial programs having similar consciousness and harm-avoidance as humans."

The Operator recalls the androids marching to their death as commanded by Nacho.

Cass turns left again, and the pair walk along the back side of the water treatment machines. "It took him a long time to find what part of the city his mother ran to with her android lover. But, as soon as he did, he set up the surveillance community outside, searching for the entrance. We could get past it at first, but over time it grew to what you witnessed yourself."

"Why didn't he just look up the water treatment facility's location?"

"To be honest, I don't know. I don't think he knows that's what we started as, so he never looked at the service grid. Thankfully, because it wouldn't have taken him long to gain access."

"So he wants to eliminate every android?"

"Not quite—much worse. Identify and *control* every android. Completely." Cass stops and points to the first balcony. There, an inert old man sits in one of two chairs, his arm around the other and his head against his chest. "I'd imagine he'd be eliminated though, if Howl ever got in here."

"Who's he?" the Operator asks.

"That's the man Howl's mother ran away with."

CHAPTER TWENTY-FIVE

THE OPERATOR SETTLES into the daily rhythms of the android refugee camp as infuriating days go by below the surface. He wakes up each day ready for the trip to wherever Gabi's being held, and his mood sours throughout the day as no news about her location emerges.

"Everyone's looking for her," Cass assures him. Their conversation ends in an argument every time they speak, with the Operator claiming he'll leave on his own and Cass obstinate in her opinion that they should wait.

"If Howl knows you're searching for her, he'll make sure we never find her. She'll turn up," she says during one of their conversations, one of many in the shadows of the water treatment machines.

"They took her days ago!" the Operator says. "Who knows what they're doing to her."

"We'll get her back, just be patient."

"Easy for you to say, you don't have some scientist running tests on you."

Miguel still being in a coma doesn't help the Operator's nerves. When he's not eating, sleeping, or helping with the water treatment efforts, he's at his friend's side. He doesn't say much beyond simple greetings and promises to be back when he leaves, but being with Miguel in the infirmary helps him feel like he's doing *something*, when the rest of his existence leaves the taste of unwelcome impotence in his mouth.

The androids from the upper levels trickle back as the work week draws to a close in the upper levels. None come through the main entrance, not yet knowing it's accessible. Instead, they come in through a metal grate behind the water treatment machines that access the sewers. It's kept locked at all times—when someone arrives, they wait for admittance after hitting the bars with a metal bar kept on the ground. None of the dozens that arrive report knowledge of Gabi's whereabouts; all but one knew they were searching for her in the first place.

"How could you not know?" the Operator says, standing next to Cass during the android debriefing. There are six new android arrivals standing in a row outside the metal grate, now locked after the workers returned to the camp.

"Where I work's a dead zone," the android says as an explanation. He's the same height as the Operator but looks like he's Miguel's age. His belly pushes against his thin white T-shirt, and his thin black beard has gray flecks throughout.

"Shoji works in one of the government offices on the forty-second," Cass explains.

"One of a handful above the twentieth," Shoji adds, with pride.

"Our transmissions are a crapshoot that high," Cass says.

The Operator keeps his eye on Shoji while the rest of the androids report they couldn't find out any information about Gabi either.

"You trust that guy?" the Operator asks Cass when it's just the two of them.

She knows he's talking about Shoji. "He's one of the camp's

veterans, that's why he's up so high in the first place. Been working the surface for years, and always brings back money or something useful for the rest of us."

"Always that high?"

"Not always. He took the place of the older android Dr. Howl's mother fell in love with."

"Howl came from the forty-second? I assumed he'd be from higher up."

"He worked his way up. Tried convincing his mom to go higher with him too, but she wouldn't budge. He found out why when she left his dad."

The Operator turns and watches Shoji walk into the cafeteria. "Where was he before he took that position?"

"You're so suspicious! And for no reason—I'd trust Shoji with my life."

"Where was he?"

"A bunch of levels. He prefers working, so he'd take the skin of androids who didn't want to work that week, even if it was his week off. Now, he doesn't miss a week—he's the only one who leaves for that particular job."

The Operator tells Cass he's feeling hungry. "I'm going to get something to eat," he says.

"And keep an eye on your new best friend," Cass says, laughing. "Enjoy."

The Operator gets in the back of the line and watches Shoji take his tray and sit alone. After grabbing a tray for himself, he takes a seat at the back of the cafeteria, facing everyone else in the room but with a particular focus on the new arrival. When Shoji finishes his portion, the android returns to the line and gets a second helping, scooped into the same bowl by the cafeteria worker with a smile. After his meal, Shoji cleans up after himself and walks out. The Operator follows, taking note of where he disappears from view on one of the balconies above.

The other android arrivals also don't know anything about Gabi's location. "If nobody comes back with information, I'm going up myself," the Operator says after the returning androids give their reports.

"There's nobody else coming back," Cass says.

"That's everyone?"

"Maybe a few more I'm not thinking about, but that's mostly everyone."

The Operator storms off to the infirmary. Cass follows him.

"Hopefully you'll be awake by the time I get back, and I'll have some good news for you," the Operator says to an unconscious Miguel.

"You can't leave," a desperate Cass says. "This affects us all."

"You're not doing anything!"

"There's nothing to do!"

"Well, we have to do something! Who knows what they're doing to her. It's only a matter of time before we're all at risk. Including you."

"You don't think I know that! This is about more than the girl—it's about all of us."

"I don't need you. I don't need anyone."

"You don't have a choice. You walk in there alone, Butler will eat you alive. Even you can't outshoot him, and you know it."

The Operator stares at Cass then starts walking out without saying another word to Miguel. Cass grabs his arm.

"Promise you won't do anything stupid."

The Operator pulls his arm away and storms out.

He doesn't leave. Knowing Cass is right and feeling neutered, he walks up the first flight of stairs and to the portion of the balcony where he sleeps. Despite the early hour, he lies down, staring at the bottom of the balcony above.

At some point, well after the camp has died down for the night, he turns to his side and focuses his attention on where Shoji rests. Despite Cass's faith in her comrade, he can't get rid of the nagging suspicion he feels towards the jovial man. How could he not know about the search for Gabi?

The camp's main lights dim, and the Operator lies awake, still staring. Hours go by and sleep doesn't visit. He thinks his imagination's playing tricks on him when he sees Shoji stand up and walk from his spot on the balcony to the stairs, not a care in the world and ignoring the rest of the camp.

The Operator wonders if the man has special access to the cafeteria, is going back for a midnight snack. Instead, Shoji starts climbing the stairs. Confused, and now certain he's not imagining the situation, the Operator gets up from his bed and walks around the balcony to the stairs. Shoji's unhurried footsteps ring out from high above him.

Taking two steps at a time, and careful not to make too much noise with his footsteps, the Operator follows. He gets to the top and scans the surrounding balconies. There's no sign of movement. A dull thud rings out from the end of the corridor that accesses the parking garage. The Operator peeks around the wall.

The android at the end of the corridor lies in a heap on the ground. Shoji holds a metal pipe in his left hand. The attacker turns around and a wicked smile passes over his lips as he watches the Operator break out into a run. He presses the button, and the metal door begins opening.

The Operator pulls out his blaster. When the Operator is mere steps away from Shoji, the man turns around and faces the Operator in an attacking stance, his pipe held chest height.

"Why?" the Operator asks.

Shoji, every trace of geniality gone, sets his jaw. Then, his head jerks left to right, his eyes rolling to the back of his head.

The metal doors stop opening and the concrete doors begin parting. Beyond the door are a team of androids in gray compressions suits with their weapons drawn. The Operator starts firing, taking the heads off five before they even know what's happening. By the time they have their blasters at their shoulders, he's rolling to the left, towards Shoji and the door's button.

Shoji rushes forward, swinging the pipe down on the Operator's back.

White flashes in front of the Operator's eyes in a moment of pain. When he recovers, he sticks his blaster under Shoji's chin and fires, sending a stream of sparks and wires to the ceiling.

Two androids in the parking garage start coming through the doors, eager for their chance at ending the Operator's existence. The button on the wall is within reach but he keeps it open, hell-bent on exacting revenge—the perfect release for his pent-up frustration. The Operator takes out the kneecaps of the two closest androids before firing a shot into one of their heads. The second, bent over after his leg's been compromised, becomes a shield when the Operator puts his shoulder into his gut and drives him forward. When the Operator stands up and dumps the body, he shoots him in the head as he falls.

There are three more androids in the parking garage, running for refuge behind nearby cars. When one on his right pops up, the Operator holds his gun out at chest height without turning his body and fires, hitting the android between the eyes. The other two are hidden behind a car in the same row where he took cover from Butler's shots with Miguel. The four android corpses from the previous shoot-out are still on the pavement.

"Did you think you could just come in here—" the Operator shouts, punctuating the final word with a shot against the car they're using for protection.

"Like you're one of us—" another shot, now within arm's reach of the car.

"And nobody would fight back?" An android sticks his head up. The Operator buries a shot in his forehead while climbing onto the trunk of the car. The sole remaining android, his back against the car, doesn't know the Operator looks down on him from above.

The Operator jumps down on the security android, forcing him onto his stomach. Kneeling on his back, he fires a series of shots into the android's neck, severing his head. When he's done, he stands up and kicks the head across the pavement. It hits the wall with a thud.

After one final glance around the parking garage, ensuring there aren't any more androids, the Operator walks back through the concrete and metal doors, pushing the button as Cass turns the corner. Her eyes fall on Shoji and she looks at the Operator, confused.

"He tried letting them in," the Operator says as the doors start closing. He takes the android security scraps and throws them into the parking garage while there's still space between the doors. Shoji, despite his betrayal, doesn't deserve the same fate.

"And I know where Gabi is."

CHAPTER TWENTY-SIX

THE OPERATOR DESCENDS the stairs while the rest of the android refugee camp is still silent, with no alarm raised and the lights still dimmed. Cass is the sole person who checked on the door's unscheduled opening—nobody else knows how close they all were to annihilation. Above him, Cass's footsteps ring out as she begins descending the stairs as well, but they disappear before she catches up to him.

On the ground level, with the machines whirring and water rushing in the background, the Operator looks up and sees Cass on a balcony a few levels from the top, walking back towards the staircase. Behind her is an android reminiscent of a heavyset teenager. The pair walks back up the stairs and disappears from view. Cass reemerges at the top of the stairs and places the inert android's body at the top of the stairs before walking down to where the Operator waits leaning against one of the water treatment machines.

"I can't believe Shoji would do this," Cass says when she reaches him.

"You said he's been working above the surface for years, right?"

"Years."

"And never had an issue before? Never been discovered?"

"Not once."

"It's because Dr. Howl found out he was an android and took control."

Realization paints Cass's features. "And he sent him back down here to let the androids in!"

The Operator nods. "We're lucky Butler wasn't with them."

"Wait—do you think Shoji sent out the door's location too?" Cass says, pacing.

"If he didn't, I'd bet one of the androids in the parking garage did. It's only a matter of time before they're here."

Cass puts her hands up to her head and weaves her fingers through her hair. "We need to wake everyone up and prepare our defenses."

"Or . . ." the Operator says. He waits until he has Cass's attention. "We take the fight to them and rescue Gabi in the process."

"Gabi? What's the girl have to do with this?"

"How do you think Shoji was discovered? You said yourself, he never had any problems."

"That girl did it!" Cass says, enraged. "And you want to rescue her?"

"*That girl* is just a child. It's not her fault."

"She could've kept her mouth shut."

"How was she supposed to know? There are many androids doing odd jobs that high up. There's no way she could've known he was hiding."

"And how can *you* know the way she thinks?" Cass hisses.

"I can't. But she never once acted like I was different, or less than," the Operator says, his words tinged with sadness.

Cass continues pacing but slows down. Calmer, she says,

"So, you suggest we abandon the camp and go to where Shoji worked?"

"Not abandon, just take some people up to the forty-second. She's got to be there, somewhere."

Cass looks at the Operator before closing her eyes and hanging her head. "I'll let the others decide if they want to go with you." She walks into a room next to the cafeteria and an instant later the lights return to full brightness. After coming back out, she stands in the middle of the room and yells at the top of her voice, "Wake every single member of the camp up! There's been an attack."

Within minutes, every android stands on the bottom level, dwarfed by the water treatment machines. Some are short, some tall; some thick and some slender; there are males, females, and gender neutral; with skin and without; and every possible step in the android evolutionary ladder, from basic, stiff-jointed individuals to ones almost as advanced as the Operator. When they're all gathered, some still tired and others bright and cheerful, Cass climbs the stairs to the first balcony's level and commands their attention.

"One of our own was corrupted by Dr. Howl," she begins. Some of the androids around the older-looking android Dr. Howl's mother ran away with look at him; others avoid staring on purpose.

"Shoji," Cass says, emotionless. A murmur passes through the crowd, with several androids hanging their heads. The cafeteria worker falls to her knees. It's obvious he was well-liked.

"Our new friend proposes we take the fight to the good doctor, and take back the girl who identified Shoji," Cass continues.

Androids around the Operator look at him as if his circuitry's corrupted. "This is just the first step," the Operator says, loud enough for all to hear. "None of us are safe if Dr. Howl finds a way to replicate her ability to identify androids at a glance."

The crowd falls silent. All of a sudden, the medical android says she'd go if Miguel wakes up in time. "We'll never be safe until she's out of his custody," she says.

"And I tend to agree with them," Cass says. "There's no point in saving the camp unless we also get Gabi back."

"You should go with him, you were security in a past life," the cafeteria android says to a tall, muscular male android. "And Shoji's friend. Avenge him."

The android looks at the Operator and nods.

"I was Shoji's friend too," a lithe woman with long hair, pointy ears, and exposed wiring on her shoulders says. "They need to pay for this."

Shoji had a lot of friends. The Operator ends up with over twenty volunteers for his mission, but by the time the ones without a reasonable background are eliminated from the group, he has eight, making himself the ninth. In addition to the two initial volunteers, there are three skinless androids who worked with the government security teams, a former Enforcer who knew Bacas, and two young men almost as advanced as the Operator—former children of a wealthy couple on the eighty-first who ran away. They all have their own blasters.

"The rest of you—it's time to prepare for their next attack! Get Stim from the cafeteria and let's get to work!" Cass proclaims before walking down the steps.

As the androids scurry away, Cass approaches the Operator and extends a hand. "Good luck," she says, shaking hands with the Operator. "They'll show you the route we take out of here and how we get between levels. You're on your own once you get to the forty-second—I hope you know what you're doing."

"We'll figure something out."

Cass turns to one of the skinless androids that joined the mission. "Shoji's body is at the top of the staircase."

The skinless android nods, then walks away.

"All right, everyone, say your goodbyes," the Operator says to his team. "We'll meet at the metal grate in twenty minutes."

In the infirmary, the medical android hovers over Miguel, checking his wound. She covers his body with the sheet when the Operator enters the room, saying she'll be right outside.

The Operator stands next to his friend and puts a hand on his shoulder. "I'll be back with Gabi. You just worry about getting better," he says. He spends the next few minutes in silence, content with existing alongside his friend without expectation. A door closing in the infirmary's main room pulls him from his reverie, and after a couple taps with his own hand on Miguel's, he leaves the recovery room.

The medical android is standing in front of the skinless android with her hands on their face while they look down right above her.

"That should do it," the medical android says, withdrawing her hands. The skinless android pulls away, their face now the color of skin. They turn to the Operator, and he sees Shoji's face and neck on an otherwise dull gray metal skeleton.

Shocked, the Operator asks why.

"So we can get onto the forty-second," the new Shoji says. They even have his voice.

"No time for the rest of the skin—we'll get it on you if you come back."

"*When* I come back," new-Shoji says with a nod.

"When," the medical android says, correcting herself. "For now, just put some clothes on. Nobody will be able to tell."

The new Shoji nods, tells the Operator he'll see him at the metal grate, and walks out.

The medical android laughs when she sees the Operator's shock. "You'll get used to it," she says.

"Not sure I ever will."

After leaving the infirmary, he walks to the locked metal grate. Seven members of the team are already there. The skinless androids are wearing black sweatsuits, black gloves, and rubber flesh-colored masks, with black face masks covering half their faces and their hoods over their metal heads. The ninth member of their team, new-Shoji, walks up wearing the same sweatsuit and gloves, his head covered too but his face exposed.

"Everyone ready?" the Operator says.

The team all nod.

The Operator unlocks the metal grate, then looks across the room to where a nearby android is watching them leave. "Lock this behind us?" he says.

The android nods.

Inside the tunnel, the Operator turns around and asks the team which of them knows where to go.

"We all do," the second volunteer says, the exposed wiring on her shoulders now covered up. "Or, we should," she adds, looking around. Every other android nods.

"I'll be in the middle," the Operator says.

With four androids in front of him and four behind, the Operator travels through the tunnel to the midline, then to the basement of a nearby building. They end up in an elevator shaft. "Reaches all the way to the hundredth," one of the runaway android siblings says with mischievous pride, like the android refugee camp stole the shaft and hid it in plain sight.

They start climbing. When they get to the forty-first level, new-Shoji, at the front of the group, tells the rest of them he'll go inside and come back and let them in. He injects a vial of Stim into his arm before climbing into a vent right above the forty-second level and disappearing from view.

"He'll drop down outside of the security checkpoint then come in using Shoji's face," the former Enforcer says.

The minutes drag by. The Operator thinks about Gabi, hoping she's safe, and Miguel, wondering if his friend will wake up. The urge for action starts as a minor itch in the base of his stomach but crawls up his spine and over his skull until his eyes squint, burning with a subdued craving for retribution. When he feels like he can't take any more waiting, the elevator doors open and Shoji's face appears.

"Come on in, everyone," he says with a smile before standing up. He holds the doors open and watches as everyone but the Operator takes a dose of Stim before climbing through and under the chain across the doors that proclaims the elevator is broken.

"It'll never be repaired," one runaway sibling says to the other. They both laugh.

A hall stretches out in front of them, with numerous metal doors with adjacent keypads along it. There's another, longer, on their right, with no doors—the right-side wall is one continuous segment and the left has breaks in it where other halls begin. Gabi could be in any of them. All of a sudden, the lights cut out, replaced by a dull red glow. Then, an alarm begins blaring and the sirens on every corner where two corridors meet start flashing bright red lights.

"What's going on?" the muscular android, the first volunteer, says.

"Small problem," new-Shoji says, sucking air in against his clenched teeth while holding up his hand, index finger and thumb almost touching. "The guards recognized me, said I shouldn't be here."

"How'd you get past them?"

"Well . . ." new-Shoji says, tapping the blaster at his side as a khaki-wearing security guard turns the corner and starts firing.

CHAPTER TWENTY-SEVEN

THE OPERATOR PULLS out his blaster and fires at the first guard to turn the corner ahead. The shot hits the man in the chest, and he stumbles back while discharging his gun into the ceiling behind the group. In shock, the guard brings his free hand up over his chest before pulling it away and inspecting his spilt blood.

The rest of the infiltration team duck and scurry into the long hall on their right. The Operator saunters over to the rest of his team as the shot guard collapses on the ground. More guards turn the corner, one pulling their comrade back to safety. Their shots hit the wall as far left as possible, just missing their target.

"Heard one of them say before I shot him that they couldn't reach Howl so far below," new-Shoji reports.

"Let's hope Butler's with him," one of the runaways says.

Another group of three guards appears from around a corner ahead and the group makes quick work of the threat, eliminating them with a barrage of blaster fire. The Operator looks back into the hall he just left, shooting two guards before letting the remaining three retreat.

"Anyone know which way?" the slender woman asks.

"On the opposite corner from where we are," new-Shoji says. Everyone looks at him, questioning how he knows. "I saw a map on their computer screen," he says with a shrug.

"Let's go," the Operator says with a nod down their current corridor.

The group sets off on a jog, with the Operator running backwards and firing continuous shots at the corner near the elevator. He runs into the group the first time they stop to check for guards before crossing a new hall, and from then on the muscular android keeps a hand on the Operator's back, stopping him when the rest of the group does.

They make their way to the end of the hall the Operator guesses runs the entire length of the building. With two halls left between them and the end, the guards from where the infiltrators first emerged from the elevator turn the corner in a group, rushing into the space with reinforcements.

In a flash, before the guards can take aim, the Operator plans out the series of shots that will take down every one of his pursuers. Six shots for six guards, prepared for if there are more on the way.

He pulls the trigger and nothing happens.

"Need some help back here!" the Operator yells.

The muscular android turns and a shot hits him in the shoulder. He starts firing like a madman, a wild spray that hits one of the guards and scatters the others, with the rest of the shots buried in the walls and ceiling.

The infiltration team turns onto one of the two halls between them and the end of the building. More metal doors, with keypads next to each, stretch off into the distance. The Operator hits his blaster with the palm of his hand, pulling the trigger while aiming at the floor between each strike as a test.

"Here, we'll switch," one of the skinless androids with a rubber mask says. "You're a better shot than me."

The Operator doesn't hesitate. He takes the new blaster, feels its weight, and holds it up while looking down the sights. It's a newer blaster than his own trusted firearm, with a customized grip, trigger, and sights. "This will do just fine," he says with a smile.

The android now in possession of the Operator's weapon holds it up, aims at the wall, and fires. A hole in the wall appears, with black burn marks around the edges. They look at the Operator; both shrug.

Blaster fire from the security guards rains down on where the infiltration team disappeared. The Operator, with a sly grin to his comrades, stands with his back against the wall. He holds up three fingers, then two. The blasters stop firing when he has just one finger in the air.

With a jump, he launches himself into the corridor, orienting himself horizontal. Blaster fire strikes three guards before any of them get a single shot off, and two more absorb shots while their own shots miss. The Operator hits the ground, shoulder first. The final guard takes a shot to the chest and falls.

The rest of the Operator's team turns the corner with blasters drawn while the Operator stands back up. They rush forward and eliminate the two guards who aren't incapacitated with swift shots to the head. In a serene moment, with no guards after them and the sirens still blaring overhead, the group turn and look at the Operator in awe.

"You're hit," the muscular android says, pointing at the Operator's thigh.

The Operator looks down. There's a growing wet spot on his dust-covered black pants, darker than the rest.

"Luck was bound to run out eventually." He tests his leg out by shifting his weight to one side—it hurts but doesn't seem weak. With a shrug, he says, "Let's go."

The group turn and jog towards the end of the corridor,

careful before crossing the penultimate aisle. They turn at the wall and, with nowhere else to go, continue down the last aisle. There's a door in their path where a door shouldn't be if the hall runs the length of the building. They run past the metal doors on their left; there are none on their right.

They pause before bursting through the roadblock, everyone but the Operator preparing for a firefight by taking a second dose of Stim. Then, the muscular android throws his shoulder against the door and stumbles into a massive open space.

Rows of loaded pallets stand between them and the open space in the middle. It's a port for hovercrafts, three levels high, extending most of the way to the other side of the building. The entire side of the building is gone, exposing the interior to the open air. Hovercrafts zip through the air outside, illuminated from behind by a flashing neon billboard of chopsticks pulling noodles from a cup on the far building. In the middle of the dock, the largest hoverbarge the Operator's ever seen sits with its rear door open as mechanized metal suits twice the height of humans place pallets into the cargo hold. Smaller hoverbarges and various sleek crafts are parked around it.

"Shoji never said anything about getting up above the forty-second," the muscular android says, his eyes on the above levels. There are steps leading up to doors two levels above their own.

"Maybe he never came in here," the slender woman says.

"He missed out," new-Shoji says.

A mechanized suit walks down the ramp leading into the hoverbarge and walks towards the android refugees. There's a person inside, visible through clear glass. The group all hide behind pallets, waiting. The mechanized suit lifts the pallet the runaways hid behind, exposing them. They scurry to another pallet before their protection is high enough off the ground that the suit's operator can see them. Everyone waits with bated breath.

The mechanized suit turns around and takes the cargo back to the hoverbarge.

"You said she's being held on the opposite corner . . . was that on this level?" the Operator asks new-Shoji.

"I think so? I'm not sure. I didn't see anything about this place," new-Shoji says, his finger twirling in the air.

"I think they're separate guards," the slender woman says. "Look." She points across the port at the two uppermost corners. The posted androids wear dark gray compression.

"And there's two outside that door across from us," one of the skinless androids says.

"Dr. Howl's team," the Operator says.

"What should we do?" the muscular android says.

"We could distract them," one of the runaways says. "Then you can go into that area behind the guards by yourself," he adds, pointing to the Operator.

"What should we do?" the former Enforcer asks.

The brothers look at each other and smile. "Follow our lead."

On their instruction, the Operator makes his way around the pallets on the side of the port farthest from the city's flow of fresh air. The androids in gray compression, blaster rifles in hand and pointed down, stand without moving, their eyes unblinking. All of a sudden, a crash on the ramp leading into the hoverbarge rings out, filling the entire port. The Operator risks a peek and sees one of the mechanized suits lying on its side. As he watches, another suit falls, this one carrying a pallet in its hand. The resulting crash rattles the ground.

On each side of the ramp are one of the runaway siblings, with a fabric strap pulled tight between them.

Every android in the port takes aim and fires at the siblings, who find refuge beneath the ramp. Mechanized suits fall down throughout the port, knocked over by other members of the infiltration team. The Operator looks at the two androids guarding the door—they haven't moved.

"It's Stim!" one of the runaways yells. The Operator sees the muscular android rip open a pallet in the corner on the same wall. Taking two vials, one in each hand, he injects one into each forearm. He looks at the Operator, his eyes wide. Then, peeking over the torn pallet ahead of him, he finds the two android guards.

With a smile, he crawls the length of the port, past the Operator, and down the length of the wall opposite where they entered. Close to his targets, he stands up with a roar and bowls over the two android guards with his shoulder before dropping back down onto all fours and scurrying away behind rows of pallets closer to the open side of the building.

The two infuriated androids follow him, their blasters at their shoulder.

The Operator doesn't waste any time. He runs to the door and grabs the handle. It's locked. He throws his shoulder against it but it doesn't budge. Then, he pulls out his blaster, shooting the lock. The metal is impenetrable—the shots leave little more than black marks. He turns around and watches the chaos unfold behind him.

Some of the mechanized suits have made it to all fours, and some still lie inert. Smoke rises up from somewhere behind the hoverbarge, and androids in gray compression suits are both running down the stairs and shooting from above.

Frustrated, the Operator shoots the keypad next to the door. A click emanates from the door and it sways on its hinges, open.

The Operator rushes through and closes the door behind him. He's in a science lab, large workstations interspersed throughout. Some are near various cutting-edge industrial machines; others have rows upon rows of small containers stacked up on one side of the table. A series of fume hoods line the wall on his left, and rooms sealed with glass are along the wall on his right.

Running along the right wall, he's surprised at what Dr. Howl keeps for prisoners. There is a skinless security-style android and an archaic type not seen since the start of the vertical revolution. He stops when he sees a sleeping midliner, wondering how the creature got so high above the surface. In the fourth room is an android that looks just like him. They stare at each other for a moment, the prisoner's hands against the glass, before the imprisoned version points to the fifth and final cell.

Inside the cell, her back against the glass, is Gabi.

When she hears a knock on the glass, Gabi turns around and looks at the relieved Operator. She doesn't realize it's not the clone—she shrugs and shakes her head, asking without words what the android wants.

The Operator taps his chest twice. "It's me!" he yells.

Gabi can't hear him.

He drops to his knees and places his hands against the glass, his forehead between them and eyes cast down. When he looks up, Gabi has tears in her eyes.

"I knew it," she mouths.

CHAPTER TWENTY-EIGHT

GABI POINTS to a raised platform along the wall past her cell. On it sits a stand supporting a computer with a tangle of attached wires. She puts her hands against the glass as the Operator stands up, walks over, and accesses the computer. Moments later, the glass drops down into the floor in front of her cell. She rushes out and wraps her arms around the Operator's midsection, squeezing him tight.

The rest of the cells are also open; every prisoner inches forward, uncertain about their newfound freedom. They all watch as the Operator pats Gabi's back twice and pries her off of him.

"Let's get out of here," he says to her with a hint of a smile on his lips.

She nods with tears in her eyes.

"All of you, grab something to defend yourself with and come on," the Operator says, gesturing with his chin towards the door.

The former prisoners gather at the door with an assortment of metal pipes, a fire extinguisher, and a broken flask between them. The Operator takes a soldering iron from Gabi's grasp, telling her she won't have the chance to use it. "You're with me," he says, setting it down on the nearest workstation. Then, he creeps open the door and leads the group through.

The port is in chaos. The few mechanized suits still standing are dented, with limbs bent at odd angles. One group of androids in gray compression on the other side of the port stand facing the far wall a few paces from three pallets sitting side by side, firing a continuous wave of shots at the cargo. The muscular android is in a crumpled heap near the side of the port open to the city air, and the two still-skinless androids are tied up near him, their rubber masks removed. When they see the Operator emerge with the group of prisoners, they turn towards the port's open side and begin shouting.

"Reinforcements are here!" they say in jubilation while looking outside, drawing the guard's attention away from where their comrades emerged.

"In here! Come get us!" the second captured android says to the city's air.

The security androids near the yelling captives turn and look outside, their blaster rifles held at their shoulders. Dozens of hovercrafts zip by. They watch, unsure of which vehicle has the reinforcements.

The Operator capitalizes on the momentary distraction and runs around the back side of the port with the freed prisoners, crouching behind pallets of Stim. They get to the far corner before anyone sees them.

"The prisoners are escaping!" a security android says from the walkway above the science lab's door, pointing to the Operator and his group as they take refuge behind pallets of boxes.

Realizing the captive androids created a distraction, a nearby guard shoots them both in the head. The sound of their shots blends in with the shots that rain down on the barrier between the escapees and the rest of the port.

"Surprised we lasted this long," the Operator's clone says to him.

The Operator grunts.

A fallen security guard is on the ground in front of them, a blaster still in their hand. The Operator's clone nods to the weapon. "Cover me," he says.

The Operator emerges over the pallet, using it as support for his arms while he takes aim at the guard on the walkway; they fall after one well-placed shot. Two more guards turn their attention towards him from near the hoverbarge in the middle of the port, and the Operator eliminates them with two quick shots to the head.

Meanwhile, his clone scurries forward, grabs the blaster rifle, and returns to the group, just in time to see a guard appear from the direction they came that the Operator doesn't notice. The guard aims at the Operator before a shot from the Operator's clone strikes him in the chest.

"Thanks," the Operator says.

His clone nods.

The runaway brothers, still under the hoverbarge's ramp, yell for the retreat. "Let's get out of here!" one of them says, loud enough so everyone in the port hears. They both come crawling out from beneath the ramp, shooting the three androids pinning down their friends while shots from somewhere above the Operator rain down on them.

The Operator runs along the wall to the door they first came through, his group right behind him. At the door, the female android ushers the prisoners through while the Operator turns around and starts picking off the androids shooting down at the siblings. Each shot finds its mark, and after the first few guards fall, the rest of their comrades take cover.

After the siblings make it through the door, the woman pulls the Operator through and slams it shut.

New-Shoji, the former Enforcer, the siblings, and the woman are the sole remaining members of the rescue party on the far side of the door. The muscular android and both skinless androids that wore rubber masks are missing. "We'll come back for them," new-Shoji says.

The Operator wonders how many of those present believe the statement.

"I've seen you before, working for them," Gabi says, looking at new-Shoji.

"I'm on your side now," he says, smiling.

They start running back in the direction they came, over the bodies of androids lying in the hallway, their limbs bent at odd angles.

"We made sure we could still get back out when you got into the lab," the female android says.

"Smart," the Operator says.

The group almost make it to the end of the hall before the androids burst through the door leading to the port behind them. Anticipating the coming gunfire, the Operator pushes Gabi down into a crouch next to the wall, keeping himself between her and the attackers. "Keep moving!" he yells.

The Operator's clone turns around and starts firing, standing in the middle of the aisle, while the rest of the group follow Gabi's lead and run bent over. The first wave of androids are gone when the Operator stands back up with his blaster drawn.

"Let's go," the clone says.

The group turn down the longer corridor that runs the length of the building and run past the aisles where rows of metal doors extend into the distance. The midliner struggles, the stunted growth of his lungs and legs making keeping up with the group difficult. The elevator shaft is far ahead, on the left side of the aisle. "We came through here on the way up," a breathless Gabi says. "There are guards."

"We know," the Operator replies.

As if they heard the girl mention them, a group of three khaki-wearing guards turn the corner onto their path. The trio hesitate when they see how many escapees are running towards them, and in that moment the Operator and his clone eliminate all three. The group continue, leaping over their bodies.

The elevator shaft is close—there's just one more aisle to go —when another, larger force emerges. The female android pulls the forward members of the group into the hallway perpendicular to their own and the rest of the group follows. The early-version android can't change direction fast enough and receives dozens of shots all over his body, sparks flying from exposed wires.

Gabi stares with wide eyes before the Operator grabs her shoulder and turns her away.

The Operator lies prone on the ground, crawls forward, and peeks around the edge. There's now a portable barrier set up across the width of the hall, and more than a dozen khaki-wearing guards behind it. The top of the elevator shaft, the doors still open, is visible above their heads. Just then, a shot lands next to the Operator's head from behind. He turns around and sees gray-compression-wearing androids running towards his position.

"What are we going to do?" new-Shoji asks. "There's no way we can get to the elevator shaft."

The ancient android, lying on the ground where the two halls intersect and looking in the direction of the elevator shaft, makes a gurgling noise. It turns its head to the group and manages just one word: Butler.

The Operator's stomach turns: if Butler came from the shaft, he must have made it through the camp.

"No way," the former Enforcer says. He peeks around the corner without thinking about the shots coming from both sides. In the end, neither group of guards matters—his head explodes at the same time a booming shot erupts, magnified by the close quarters.

"Run!" the Operator says. The group travels down the hall they're in, the female android first and the Operator and his clone bringing up the rear. When the Operator hears footsteps turn the corner behind him, he yells, "Turn!" to the android in front. She turns right, and they continue down another hallway perpendicular to the previous. They cross a hall with gray-compression-wearing androids traveling in the opposite direction at the other end; they're gone by the time the guards begin firing.

After a series of twists and turns, through which the Operator and his clone take turns laying cover fire, the group burst through a door blocking their path and emerge back into the port, with the side open to the city in front of them. The mechanized suits stand along the edge, spaced out so their ranks cover the entire distance with nothing but open air behind them.

Clapping from the left side of the port draws the group's attention. It's Dr. Howl, standing alone on the walkway right above the lab. "I see you've found your counterpart," he says with a nod to the clone.

The clone puts his blaster up to his shoulder. Dr. Howl nods, disappointed, then taps his watch. All of a sudden, the Operator's clone, the midliner, and the skinless security android all drop to the ground, dead. Dr. Howl laughs. "Kill switches, in case they didn't follow orders. Gabi would've gotten one too, as soon as I could figure out whether it would alter her ability."

The Operator pulls his own blaster up and starts firing at Dr. Howl, who rushes into an adjacent room.

A volley of nearby gunfire pulls the Operator's attention

back to the group. It originated from the siblings. "The guards are here!" they say, closing the door behind them. They lean their backs against it and jolt forward when the guards push from the opposite side.

"To the hoverbarge!" the Operator says, pointing to the massive craft that dwarfs those around it. "We'll fly our way out of here." Then, turning to the siblings, he says, "I'll tell you when."

The Operator, Gabi, the female android, and new-Shoji all run across the port as a massive wall begins closing behind the mechanized suits, blocking the city beyond. The Operator sees Dr. Howl looking at them through a window, smiling and pointing to the closing wall. Everyone but the Operator climbs the ramp leading onto the hovercraft. Standing alone at the bottom, the Operator waves at the siblings. In unison, they run forward and the door behind them flies open.

The Operator pulls the trigger as fast as physics allows. Android after android falls, their heads exploding in a spray of sparks and parts.

The siblings get on, followed by the Operator, and the ramp begins closing. Shots from the androids pour into the interior through the disappearing available space. Through a window, the Operator sees Butler emerge at the head of the khaki-wearing guards from the door the infiltrators came through on their first trip to the port, on the wall opposite Dr. Howl. His booming shots join the flurry hitting the side of the vehicle, creating convex dents on the craft's interior.

"Fly this thing straight to the lower levels," the Operator yells to the siblings. "I'll hold them off as long as I can."

The androids from the camp all stare at him, confused. "Go!" the Operator yells, and the siblings run into the cabin.

"No!" Gabi yells, the sole person who understands the

implications of his statement. She grabs the Operator around the waist. The female android pulls her back.

The Operator gets down on one knee. "They'll get into a hovercraft and chase us the second we leave."

The hoverbarge lurches forward. "Let's get out of here!" one of the siblings says.

The Operator brushes Gabi's hair back from her face. "Cass and the others will keep you safe, but you have to get to them first." He stands up and walks to the door on the side opposite Butler and opens it. The vehicle approaches a parked, bright red hovercraft as the wall ahead creeps closed, soon blocking access to the city. The Operator turns to Gabi for the last time.

"Always knew I'd be leaving the city after I saved you," he says. Then, with his blaster in hand, he jumps.

CHAPTER TWENTY-NINE

THE HOVERBARGE BOWLS over three mechanized suits as it leaves the port. They make no efforts at saving themselves and fall over the edge. The hoverbarge teeters on the port's edge for a moment and follows the suits, plunging towards the lower levels.

The wall between the port and the city air beyond continues closing while the Operator hides behind the red hovercraft. Shots from the androids wearing gray compression suits rain down on his protection from the deepest side of the port, and more from the combination of Butler and the khaki-wearing security forces strike the side of the hovercraft. The people in the mechanized suits all stare at the Operator, protected by thick glass, as the door closes with a dull thud behind them. Some of them stumble backwards into the wall after being struck by errant shots, but their suits protect them, and they return to their post.

Dr. Howl looks down at the Operator and bangs his hands on the glass, screaming. The Operator holds his gun at chest height and a thin smile passes over his lips. He peeks around the back end of the hovercraft and eliminates the few androids that dared exposing themselves for a better shot. Then, he makes a break for the wall beneath Dr. Howl, running past the muscular android's inert body before diving behind the nearby pallets.

All of a sudden, the mechanized suits all open at once and their human operators spill out, guns in hand. They're all wearing sweat-stained plain white T-shirts and navy blue pants, with heavy work boots. The one closest to the Operator rushes forward in anger, his gun held straight out—the Operator eliminates the threat with a shot to the middle of his chest, a red hole appearing before the man falls down. The rest of the workers take cover behind hovercrafts, pallets, or their own suits.

Butler's booming shots are identifiable over the rest; each one lands on the Operator's protection with a worrying penetrating sound. There's a pattern to his shots—he fires six times before a momentary pause. After a round of six that sound as if they will pierce through the boxes on the pallet, the Operator takes cover behind another. The concentrated fire follows.

A shot whizzes past the Operator from the corner. He finds the shooter and dispatches him with a shot placed right between his eyes. Then, he runs the length of the wall and takes the corner for himself. Peeking around his cover, he eliminates six androids with a rapid series of shots before chancing a look at the rest of the port. Butler's in the middle, where the hoverbarge sat moments before. He looks right at the Operator and concentrates his fire at his target's location.

The pinned-down Operator alternates between looking down both walls, making sure no androids, security guards, or workers appear and eliminating the odd individual who takes the risk. Butler's shots continue getting closer until, after a typical pause, they don't return. The rest of the gunshots no longer rain down on the Operator's location—he hears them strike metal in the middle of the port.

Looking over the edge of the pallet, he sees a mechanized

suit holding Butler in the air from behind the moment before it slams him to the ground. The two-gunned android lands with a heavy thud while his comrades pepper the suit with gunfire. The muscular android sits inside the suit, a look of pure rage mixed with pain painted over his face. The suit steps forward and stands over Butler, bending over with his arms extended. Butler turns over and fires two simultaneous shots, one from each arm, at the mechanized suit. The glass shatters with a loud crack and the back of the suit blows away in a wave of sparks and debris. The mechanized suit falls to the ground backwards as if in slow motion.

The Operator shoots Butler three times in quick succession. The android flinches each time a shot strikes his body but doesn't fall.

At the same time, a glancing shot strikes the Operator on his left side—an eager worker who capitalized on the distraction. He rushes forward and is stopped in his tracks by the Operator's retaliatory fire, falling to the ground with a hole in his forehead.

The Operator shifts his weapon to his left hand and feels the wound. It isn't deep enough to matter. He wipes his hand on his pants and grabs his blaster with his dominant arm once more as Butler shoots the mechanized suit lying on the ground in the center of the port, making sure the muscular android never wakes up again. Then, the enhanced android turns his attention back to the Operator's corner, along with everyone else in the port.

"Kill him!" Dr. Howl yells from the walkway, having emerged from the control room. The Operator derives a large dose of pleasure knowing he's become such a thorn in the man's side, and he hopes the hoverbarge has made it down to the lower levels without crashing. He has no idea how he will stop Butler. His guns don't work against the enhanced android, and in any battle between the two of them the one who can shoot two guns just by thinking about pulling the trigger has the distinct advantage.

The Operator shoots three more androids and two more workers that try walking along the wall towards him before chancing another look at Dr. Howl. He almost short-circuits from shock when he sees who stands behind the scientist—it's Nacho and Pavlova's skinless concierge android, sneaking along the walkway. On the level above them, a slender individual in a white robe with a belt around their waist appears, their hair in a ponytail: Druid, from the Sect.

Just then, the lights go out. The port descends into madness.

Muffled footsteps pour in from every side. Then, the screams begin, followed by frenetic gunfire. The Operator capitalizes on the absolute darkness by changing his position, setting up behind the pallets below Dr. Howl. Above him, he hears the scientist scream for help before his body strikes the metal walkway with a thud. Two other bodies descend on the scientist and his screams die out.

Shots from Butler's gun appear as long flashes of fire in the middle of the port, each one coming after the sound of the butt of his gun striking a body in his vicinity. They erupt from random locations around his body as his arms flail out, revealing retreating white robes while he keeps any Sect attackers from getting too close. Butler roars, a mixture of rage and impotence.

The Operator understands Butler's frustration. Shooting is also impossible for him in the dark, and there's a chance he hits a member of the Sect if he even tries shooting where he thinks Butler is standing. All of a sudden, Druid's words echo in his head, as if the man's saying them right in his ear: "There will come a time when guns won't solve your problems."

The sound of the butt of a gun striking bone pulls the Operator from his memory. Despite not becoming proficient in the Sect's style of hand-to-hand combat, he can't keep letting them get in harm's way without helping. He holsters his weapon and walks beyond the protection offered by the pallets, heading straight to the origin of Butler's wild shots. Stumbling against a person wearing a flowing robe, he pulls them back and pushes them away, clearing them from his path. Then, the rest of the world disappears—all he hears are Butler's heavy footsteps in front of him.

In a staggered stance, the Operator swings out with his right fist and strikes Butler on the side. It's the first punch he ever learned from Druid, and he's surprised his body remembers the stance. In response, Butler swings his right arm in a wide arc. Anticipating the retaliation, the Operator ducks, then sidesteps as Butler brings his elbow to his side and fires a shot at where the Operator stood a moment before. The added step wasn't in the Sect's arsenal of positions; it came from imagining what he would do in Butler's shoes, if he had no choice but to use his guns in close quarters.

Guessing where Butler's face is, the Operator reaches out and touches it with his left hand, gauging the distance. Then, he braces and blocks Butler's incoming left gun with his right forearm, feeling the shot erupt from the weapon the moment after it makes contact. A right cross then makes solid contact with Butler's face.

Butler stumbles back as the Operator transfers his momentum from the right-handed punch into a left spin. He ends up on Butler's right, far away from the shots Butler takes with both arms in front of him.

The Operator executes a front kick, the move Druid tried teaching him without success all those years ago, and it lands on Butler's right hip, knocking the android down. The Operator assumes the android has fallen onto his side and steps forward, planting with his right leg while kicking with his left. Butler, on one knee, hooks the Operator's left leg with his right elbow and yanks up, throwing the Operator down on the ground. Butler stands up and fires both guns into the ground where the Operator fell, but his bullets miss—the Operator rolled the second he hit the ground.

Planting his hands on the ground, the Operator spins his legs around and stands up facing Butler. For a moment, the flash of gunfire and associated noise surrounds him, the screams of stricken men overloading his senses. In a flash of understanding, Druid's purpose for living in the desert makes sense. "Nobody can afford spending the time it takes to get good when the city bombards the senses all hours of the day." He exhales and the world drowns away once more. Butler's heavy footfalls strike the ground in front of him and he hears the swoosh of the enhanced android's searching arms near his face.

The Operator ducks down, steps to the side, and lets Butler walk past him. Then, he jumps on the two-gunned android's back. Butler reaches up and behind his head. The Operator, sensing the movement in Butler's shoulders, releases his hold on his neck and exchanges it for a hand on each gun. He pulls down with all his weight, expecting Butler will fall backwards.

The android doesn't topple over—instead, he braces himself in a staggered stance and fires. Powerful vibrations through the guns' barrels threaten the Operator's grip but he doesn't let go. He wraps his legs around Butler's waist and forces the barrels of both guns towards the android's ears.

Guns can't solve all of his problems, but they can solve this one.

The Operator strikes the back of Butler's head with his own. White stars fill his vision after the clank of metal on metal. He does it again, making sure the guns stay pointed at Butler's own head. Over and over he slams his forehead into the android, waiting and hoping for something inside to give way and fire the weapons without intention. An infuriated Butler tries turning the weapons towards the Operator once more, then tries prying the weapons away from his own head with minimal success—normal humans wouldn't have the required strength to take control away from Butler, but the Operator isn't human. Butler does succeed in pulling them forward for a moment, until they're even with his cheeks, but the Operator leans back and gets the guns back against Butler's android skull, despite the smell of smoke emanating from his own shoulders.

With stars in his eyes and the sound of metal striking metal filling his ears, the Operator loses touch with reality. All he knows, all he understands, is striking the back of Butler's head with his own. He starts screaming, unaware he's making the sound, until one of his strikes hits a tiny bit lower than the rest and both guns fire right in front of his face.

CHAPTER THIRTY

A DULL RINGING fills the Operator's ears and Butler's body weighs down on his chest. The enhanced android's internal fluids combine with his long hair, sticking onto the Operator's face like a wet towel. Struggling to breathe, the Operator turns his face to the right while shoving the massive body to his left. He squirms out from beneath the android, gets onto all fours, and looks through the darkness around him.

The light from random gun flashes illuminates individual battles throughout the port. White robes, rushing forward, appear in the moments of light; each time, the gun flashes appear again higher up in the air as those holding the guns are thrown backwards. The Operator's hands detect the vibration of someone falling nearby. He crawls forward, his sense of direction lost. Someone trips over him and he lies down, unmoving, so he isn't mistaken for an enemy.

When the person who stumbled over him stands back up and runs into the darkness, he continues crawling, worthless in the fight without his sight or hearing. His hand strikes an object in his path; inspecting it, he realizes it's a pallet. The boxes on its right side are open, with vials of Stim spilling onto the ground. He considers injecting himself and getting back into the fight, but the desire soon passes—he's gone too long without the substance for a relapse. Becoming addicted once more terrifies him more than death.

The Operator sits with his back against the pallet and withdraws his gun. Soon, the appearance of gun flashes reduces, then stops altogether. The sound of grunting men, muffled footsteps, and heavy breathing begins trickling through the ringing in his ears. As he calms, the metallic taste of Butler's internal fluids appears on his tongue. He pulls his collar out, tucks his chin, and licks the inside of his shirt, then wipes the area around his mouth.

A bird call rings out from somewhere behind and above the Operator. Dozens more of the same call respond. A moment later, the lights come on.

The carnage is staggering. Almost every single khaki-wearing guard, android wearing gray compression, and worker from the mechanized suits lies on the ground, some unconscious, others groaning in pain. The others are held by members of the Sect; not a single one still has their weapon. Among the bodies on the ground are a few Sect members, identifiable by their white robes. As soon as each are spotted, their comrades who don't have hostages pull them away and take them down the hall towards the elevator.

Everyone turns their attention to the wall behind the Operator. "Tie up the survivors and cover their eyes," Druid says. His followers get to work.

The sound of three pairs of footsteps rings out from behind the Operator. He listens as they all descend the steps, and he turns to his right, waiting. The Sect leader reaches the port's floor first, followed by Nacho and Pavlova's concierge. Druid looks at the Operator out of the side of his eye, followed by the slightest of nods, before walking over to Butler. He pokes the headless android with his toe.

"You really did a number on him," Druid says, without turning around.

"Did it to himself," the Operator replies from his seated position. Nacho and the concierge turn around and look down at the Operator, not having seen him, both surprised and in awe. He's covered in blood, his shoulders and head sagging, and legs straight out against the port's floor. The blaster in his hand rests on the ground, his right palm facing up.

"You went through it," the concierge android says.

"That was one tough son of a bitch! I didn't think you had it in you," Nacho says, walking over. He bends over and slaps the Operator's foot. After a lazy tilt, it returns to neutral.

Through sheer willpower, the Operator stands up, every joint radiating pain. "Why—" he says before he feels his knees buckle. He throws a hand on the pallet next to him for support. Nacho, the closest person to him, reacts by reaching out—it lasts for a split second before the gore covering the Operator registers and he pulls away.

"Why are you here?" the Operator says once he's regained his balance.

"We came to help!" Nacho says.

"No," the Operator says, shaking his head. "Why are you *here*? How did you even find out about this place, or know we'd need help in the first place? And how do you two know each other?"

"Oh! Cass introduced us. What'd you think of her? Great, huh?" Nacho says.

Druid walks over and puts a hand on Nacho's shoulder. "Let me take this one," he says.

"Sure thing," says Nacho, backing away.

"I had some of our members track Dr. Howl after he left our

community. When he attacked you at the pool hall, they came back and convinced me you could use our help. We've been one step behind you ever since."

"You're the one who told them about Gabi in the first place," the Operator says, his tone accusatory.

"A mistake; I thought helping them would save our homes. Turns out he's more evil than I thought," he says with a sigh. "I never claimed to have all the answers—"

"So you're tracking me . . ."

"Yes, and you disappeared into the android refugee camp. We couldn't find the entrance for the longest time, until we heard a short gunfight in the parking garage."

"That's where I found them," Nacho says, leaning forward with his index finger in the air. "Came down when I heard that Howl and Butler were on their way. Thought I was warning 'em, but turns out Cass was already makin' preparations."

"And you were gone," Druid adds.

"So there we were, protecting the camp from Butler and Howl and all his droids, when they all disappear before even firing a shot—guess that's when they heard your team was breakin' in and releasin' Gabi."

"Butler came from the elevator shaft . . . I thought he went through the camp."

"Nope, they never got past the front door," Nacho says.

"Guards probably told him that's where we came from," the Operator guesses.

"We assumed there'd be more than just you here," the concierge android says, still staring in awe.

"The rest flew down to the lower levels with Gabi."

"And you stayed to give them time to escape," Druid says, nodding with paternal pride.

"No point in saving her from the lab if they're still on her tail," the Operator replies.

"What were you going to do?" Nacho says, laughing. "Butler's a handful by himself! Let alone with all these guys." Nacho tilts his head backwards, indicating all of Dr. Howl's incapacitated forces.

"Whatever I could," the Operator says.

A member of the Sect, no more than a teenager, approaches Druid from behind. "Sir, everyone's been bound and blindfolded," she says.

"Good." Druid turns to Pavlova's concierge android. "You're up."

The skinless concierge android walks back up the stairs and drags Dr. Howl's body into the control room.

"Why are they here?" the Operator asks Nacho.

"Pavlova wanted someone close to Howl. We were going to have him take the face of one of the soldiers during the battle for the camp, but once we heard everyone came back here, we guessed he'd go to the lab first and followed. And who's closer to Howl than the doctor himself?" Nacho says with a wink.

"How'd you get up here in the first place?" the Operator asks.

"The Dominguez brothers had the credentials for passing the reclaimers from some police hovercraft they shot down. Pavlova bought it off them and strapped it onto one of his own, then BAM! Next thing you know, we're on the forty-sixth."

"And then you cut the lights," the Operator says to Druid.

"The darkness is your friend when people are trying to shoot you." Druid looks at the Operator with a knowing smile. "You seemed to do all right," he says, taking another look at Butler.

"I'm more than just my guns," the Operator says, shaking his head with a chuckle.

The wall that separates the port from the city starts creeping open. Some of the mechanized suits that were leaning against it fall backwards, tumbling into city air on their way to the lower levels. Druid looks up and behind the Operator. Following the Sect leader's gaze, the Operator turns around and sees Dr. Howl standing on the balcony in front of the control room. The scientist holds an index finger up to his lips, demanding silence from everyone in the room. Druid turns around and makes sure the Sect all follows instructions.

"They'll have no idea," Nacho whispers to the Operator.

A massive hoverbarge descends from above and hovers right outside the port. Its ramp descends and comes into contact with the floor. Without a word, Druid points at the hoverbarge and the members of the Sect stream into the vehicle—their muffled footsteps are no louder than a piece of trash blowing across the ground. Druid, the Operator, and Nacho are the last into the hoverbarge. The injured members of the Sect, their white robes stained with blood, are lying on mats near the front of the craft.

Before they take off, Pavlova's android, who has taken over as Dr. Howl, runs down the stairs. "Don't think you can get away with this!"

The Operator's hand flies down to his side, grabbing his blaster; he pauses at Druid's light touch on his arm. "Watch," Druid whispers.

"You come in here, tie up my men—" the new version of Dr. Howl says before shooting the ground a number of times.

"When we get our hands on you!"

The hoverbarge pulls away from the building as Dr. Howl walks over to the closest tied-up, blindfolded person—a khaki-wearing guard. The hoverbarge's ramp draws closed.

A smiling, waving Dr. Howl leaning over to untie a captive is the last thing the Operator sees before they join the hovercraft traffic streaming between the city's buildings, illuminated by neon lights.

CHAPTER THIRTY-ONE

Both the concrete and metal doors in the parking garage open wide as the Operator approaches with the others from the port battle. Everyone that escaped before the battle waits just inside the camp: new-Shoji, the slender female android, the two runaway siblings, and Gabi, held in place by Cass. The camp leader greets them with a smile and lets Gabi go when she sees it's safe. Gabi runs to the Operator and wraps her arms around his waist.

"I can't believe you did it," Cass says to the Operator, shaking her head. She looks at Nacho and makes a show of frowning. "And you're here."

"I know you missed me," Nacho replies.

"Where's your friend?" she asks Nacho.

"He found a new gig on the upper levels—a scientist, one of the most respected in the city," Nacho says with a wink.

Cass laughs and shakes her head.

"You made it," Gabi says, looking up at the Operator with tears in her eyes.

The Operator gets down on one knee. "Takes more than a few androids to get me," he says, hugging the girl.

"Come on in," Cass says to Druid, who's still standing in the parking garage. "Where's everyone else?"

Druid shakes his head. "Still on the ship. We've got to get the bodies of those we lost back to the badlands. I just wanted to come and thank you for welcoming us into your home."

"We should be thanking you for coming to help," Cass says, shaking the man's hand. "You're welcome anytime."

Druid turns to the Operator. "Hopefully our paths cross again," he says, putting his hand on the Operator's shoulder. The Operator stands up and mimics the gesture, looks Druid in the face, and nods. Druid turns and walks away as the camp doors slide closed.

"They never got in," Cass tells the Operator as she leads the group down the hall. There are numerous barriers and stores of ammunition for a gunfight that never occurred. Gabi's left hand slides into the Operator's right; he doesn't pull away, despite his initial discomfort. "There were dozens of them in the parking garage, preparing to blast down the doors, but as we watched they all scrambled back to the surface."

"Heard about what you guys were doing to their lab," Nacho says again, slapping the Operator on the back.

The Operator despises the gesture but doesn't say a word.

A chorus of applause erupts and a collective exhale is released when the Operator emerges onto the balcony overlooking the camp's wide-open space. Far below, every android looks up and watches the Operator wave a hand to the crowd. The applause continues as he walks down the steps and joins them in the shadows of the water treatment machines. Everyone present lays a hand on the Operator's shoulder, grateful to him for saving their home.

The medical android, shorter than the rest, is at the back of the group. She waits with her hands folded in front of her and smiles when she sees the Operator notice her.

"How is he?" the Operator asks with trepidation.

"Come see for yourself," she says with a sweet smile.

Leaving the celebration behind, the Operator and Gabi follow the medical android to the infirmary. There, she pauses at the main door, saying she'll give them a minute.

The Operator pauses, hit with a wave of uncertainty about being reunited. Gabi leads him inside with a pull on his hand.

"I heard you stayed behind when they took her away," Miguel says. He's sitting propped up by two pillows. His face is gaunt but his eyes sparkle, as if he made up a massive rest deficit by sleeping for days without eating a bite.

"I did," the Operator responds.

"Could've gotten yourself killed."

The Operator nods.

Miguel smiles and raises his eyebrows, radiating smug wisdom. He turns his attention to Gabi. "She was the first thing I saw when I woke up. Standing there, holding my hand."

The Operator looks down at a blushing Gabi. "Are you a healer and never told us?"

Gabi giggles. The Operator pulls his hand away from hers and puts his arm around her shoulder, squeezing her tight. "Well, thank you."

"I didn't do anything!" she says.

"For being you."

The Operator tells Miguel all about the events that transpired while he was asleep. Gabi includes her parts of the story as well, telling what happened when she was in the upper levels. She mentions how relieved she was when she saw Shoji was still alive after divulging his true identity to Dr. Howl. The Operator doesn't mention the face swap.

Their reunion lasts until the medical android enters the room. "He still needs a few more days to recover, but he'll be good to travel soon," she says.

"Nonsense," Miguel says, propping himself up on an elbow. "I'm good to go—" He collapses back onto the pillows with a cough, his whole body tense.

"A few days," the medical android says, ushering the Operator and Gabi from the room.

The next day, Gabi wakes the Operator up and tells him Cass gave her permission to go up to the surface.

"I told her you'll come with me," she says.

"The surface? Why?" the Operator asks, sitting up.

"Because we need the sun! There's none down here."

"And she said it's all right?"

"Yup!"

Gabi walks ahead of the Operator all the way to the camp's entrance, pausing and waiting when he falls behind. The guard opens the doors, and Gabi takes the Operator's hand and pulls him through. The Operator looks into the shadows extending down the aisles, recalling the androids that shot Miguel. Gabi doesn't pay attention, and he marvels at the resiliency that childhood provides her.

She finds a suitable patch of dirt on the side of the street opposite the parking garage's entrance. There, she pulls out the packet of seeds the healer gave her with care, as if they possess the healer's magic and secrets within. She scrapes at the hard ground with her fingers, getting a thick layer of dirt beneath her nails as she digs a small hole, and lays the seeds inside the hole before covering them with dirt, just like the healer taught her. After wiping her hands on her pants, she pulls out a container of water.

"I took this from the cafeteria," she says with a guilty grin before dousing her plant.

She stands back up, and they both look down at the dirt. "Are you still planning on leaving the city?" she asks. "Cass said I can stay here, so you don't have to worry about me."

"I'll always worry about you," the Operator replies with a heavy heart. Thinking about what he would tell the girl had kept him up half the night prior. "I think I'll be staying in the city," he says. Even if he does end up leaving, there's no harm in the girl thinking he's still nearby. Just like there's no harm in her thinking Shoji survived her identification.

"That's good. I'd miss you if you left."

"I'd miss you too."

Together, they stay outside until the surrounding buildings' shadows overtake the patch of dirt.

A week later, Miguel has recovered enough to travel back to Gamma district. Amidst a renewed sense of hope and promise for the future, every android again thanks the Operator for what he did and wishes him good luck in the future. Miguel and Gabi, inseparable during the days leading up to their departure, exchange a tear-filled goodbye at the camp's entrance while Cass and the Operator watch.

When Gabi pulls apart from Miguel, the Operator gets down on one knee. "Your mother would be very proud of you," he says. She buries her face into his neck, tears streaming down her cheeks.

"Thanks again," Cass says once the Operator stands back up. She shakes his hand, then Miguel's, before making them promise they'll come back for a visit.

"You know where we are," she says.

Miguel and the Operator walk out, and the metal doors begin sliding shut. The Operator turns around halfway through the parking garage—the last thing he sees is Cass with her hand on Gabi's shoulder, both waving goodbye.

The pair of friends walk back through Sigma at a slow pace, accommodating Miguel's injury. Miguel jokes that they should visit Pavlova's club. "Have ourselves a good night," he says.

"Don't think you could handle that, amigo," the Operator says.

Miguel looks at the Operator with a smile, his emotions rendering his tongue useless. The Operator, uncomfortable with the situation's sentimentality, jokes that they should instead visit Nacho. "We can find out about that big deal he left for a few days ago," the Operator says.

"I'm too old for all that," Miguel says, shaking his head.

"We both are."

After passing through Sigma district without stopping, the pair descend into the midline. Almost halfway through the tunnel that runs between Gamma and Sigma, Miguel says he's getting tired.

"Don't know how much more I can travel today. Might have to stop for a rest," he says, a hint of mischief in his voice.

"The healer's close by. She'd know what to do," the Operator says, playing along.

"I feel bad. No reason you can't continue home . . ." Miguel says.

"Don't feel bad!" the Operator says. "It's no trouble at all. We can stop." He wishes he could see Miguel's face in the darkness.

Miguel's hand finds the Operator's back and he wraps an arm around his friend's shoulder. "Look, amigo. When a man and a woman—"

The Operator interrupts him with a laugh. "Don't worry, you're going in alone," he says. "Plus, you need to give her back the brace she gave you. You still have it, right?"

"Of course," Miguel says, reaching down and patting his leg.

The Operator doesn't need to see through the darkness to recognize his friend's beaming smile.

A short while later, Miguel spots the scent coming from the healer's home first.

At first, the Operator thinks his friend's imagination is playing tricks on him, but within another dozen steps he smells the rich earth and vegetation as well. "Now I smell it too," he says.

"Told you."

"We've got to hide your nose from Dr. Howl, in case he comes looking for you the way he did Gabi," the Operator says as they walk towards the healer's door.

Miguel pulls the door open and stands in the light. "Don't tell him I'm here," he says with a wink before closing the door and leaving the Operator in darkness.

Alone, the Operator realizes there's now no reason he can't leave the city. There's not a single person there to stop him; Miguel now has the healer, and Gabi has the android camp. He has no one, and nobody has him.

After a long while, during which he debates whether he should go back through Sigma and out the far side of the city or head back to Gamma, he puts his hand in his pocket without thinking and realizes he still has the thimble. Miguel's thimble, for a memory mirror that no longer exists. He should return it. A pang of longing for the pool hall weighing him down from inside, he turns towards Gamma and starts walking.

"Better hide those feelings, before somebody finds out," he says to himself.

COULD YOU DO ME A FAVOR?

Please help other readers learn more about this book by leaving a rating and review!

Then head over to my website authormarcoshernandez.com and subscribe to my email list. You'll hear about upcoming releases and deals you don't want to miss!

ALSO BY MARCOS ANTONIO HERNANDEZ

Android City Chronicles

The Return of the Operator

Before Anyone Finds Out

Good Enough in a Pinch

___

The Edited Genome Trilogy

Awakening

Alternative

Absolution

___

Hispanic American Heritage Stories

The Education of a Wetback

Where They Burn Books

They Also Burn People

Demons in the Golden Empire

___

Indigenous Magic

Jesus Chan and the Return of Mayan Magic

ABOUT THE AUTHOR

Marcos Antonio Hernandez writes from the suburbs of Washington, D.C. An avid reader of both fiction and nonfiction, his favorite authors are Haruki Murakami and Philip K. Dick — in that order.

Marcos graduated from the University of Maryland, College Park with a degree in chemical engineering and a minor in physics. Since graduating, he has worked as a barista, a food scientist, and a CrossFit coach.

authormarcoshernandez.com